The Indispensable Guide

to

Classic Men's Clothing

BY JOSH KARLEN AND CHRISTOPHER SULAVIK

ILLUSTRATED BY AMY LIBRA

D0089992

TATRA PRESS
NEW YORK

Library of Congress Catalog Card Number: 99-60699

ISBN: 0-9661847-1-8

Writers: Josh Karlen and Christopher C. Sulavik
Cover designed by: Regina Ranonis
Illustrator: Amy Libra
Printer: Quebecor Printing
Publisher: Tatra Press
            111 Congress Street
            Brooklyn, New York 11201

Printed in the United States of America

For Lorraine and Emily

Acknowledgment

The authors extend their sincere thanks to the many people who so generously offered their time and expertise during the research for this book. A special thanks to Stephane Houy-Towner of The Costume Institute at The Metropolitan Museum of Art.

—J.K., C.S.

CONTENTS

PREFACE

Classics never go out of style.
    —Stephen Milstein, vice president, Burlington Coat Factory

Fashion is fleeting, style is permanent.
        —Daniel Patrick Heaney, general manager, Sulka

For many men, getting dressed each morning is not the simple task it should be. They hesitate before closets overflowing with clothes, and puzzle over questions such as: Can I wear my herringbone jacket with my striped shirt? Is it appropriate to wear my button-down collar with my double-breasted suit? Is my casual outfit too casual for my office? Such questions can linger for years, even decades. And a visit to the haberdasher often devolves into a compassless journey through a wilderness of jackets, shirts and coats, prompting still more questions: Are these shoes the paragons of craftsmanship that the salesperson insists they are? Will this tie go with all the outfits I'd like to wear it with? Is this suit worth the small fortune demanded for it?

On these points, men often defer to the advice of salespeople—most of whom are competent, helpful guides. But some are ill-informed, rushed and driven by commissions. As a result, men too often end up settling for suits that fall out of fashion or that fit poorly, shoes that pinch, ties that don't agree with their taste or the rest of their wardrobe. And so, they end up back before their closets, examining their clothes with trepidation.

Why are so many men unfamiliar with the basic principles of dressing well and unable to discern quality clothing? Perhaps because many fathers don't educate their sons about things sartorial, because of their own uncertainty about clothing or a belief that the subject is trivial. However, the clothes we wear are far from trivial. Our choice of suit, coat, shoes, and so forth, powerfully influences how colleagues and acquaintances perceive us. We are judged to be successful or struggling, a conformist or a rebel, a details man or careless, based largely on our appearance. Impressions based on our clothing may be superficial, but they are inevitable. As Lord Chesterfield famously observed more than two centuries ago: "Dress is a very foolish thing, and yet it is a very foolish thing for a man not to be well dressed."

So, what does the well-dressed man wear? Men of style have always chosen classic clothing, which, like the classics we studied in school, are creations of the highest quality of craftsmanship and of aesthetic beauty. Their indefatigable elegance imparts confidence and endures changes of fashion, which, in addition, makes them a wise investment.

This book seeks to provide readers with an education in these classic men's clothes: how to recognize them among crowded shop racks, and how to wear them well. Whether you are starting a career and building your first serious wardrobe, seeking to add panache to your attire, or wishing to become an educated consumer, we believe you will find the guidelines in this book useful. If you are among those men who puzzle before their closets each morning, we hope this book will make getting dressed simple, and even enjoyable.

During the research for this book, we spoke with dozens of experts at the most venerable clothiers in the United States and abroad. We also interviewed purveyors of the finest fabrics, and spoke with the most sought-after image consultants. These experts occasionally offered divergent opinions; however, to set them down in every instance would serve no purpose. Instead, we chose to note only those contrary views that are held by a significant minority of the knowledgeable people we spoke with. Suffice it to say that for almost every opinion there is a contrasting one, and for every generality we make, there are many exceptions.

—J.K., C.S.

SUITS

The suit is no longer a suit. It's a statement.
— Garrick Anderson, designer, Garrick Anderson Sartorial Ltd.

The suit is unquestionably the most important article of clothing in a man's wardrobe. It is the uniform of businessmen from Tokyo to Moscow to New York, and will likely remain so for years to come.

The essential elements of the man's suit have changed remarkably little during the 20th century, and the contemporary suit—whether an updated Sack, a Savile Row or an Italian cut—remains an easily recognizable descendant of 19th century frock coats and lounge suits. However, there have been countless variations on the classic suits over the years, providing men with myriad choices of silhouettes, colors and fabrics. These variations—some stark, some subtle—can send very different messages about the wearer's style, his personality, what he does for a living and how successful he is. So it is prudent to consider carefully before making a substantial investment in a suit. Generally, you want to acquire suits that not only possess craftsmanship that will last many years, but that are also cut in one of the variations of the classic styles, so that they will endure passing fashions.

This chapter describes classic suit silhouettes, materials and fabric patterns. It also shows you how to recognize quality, so you can select a suit based on sound knowledge, not on the price tag or the brand label.

What are the classic suit styles?

Each suit style is distinguished by its *silhouette* (the character of a suit's lines). Three silhouettes have lasted for many decades: the *American Sack*, the *British* and the *Italian*. However, these categories are not rigid, and you will see variations when you browse through suit racks; even classics get tweaked and updated. "In the

1950s, it was perhaps easier to tell the difference between the American, British and Italian styles," says Garrick Anderson, designer for Garrick Anderson Sartorial Ltd. "Today, we still hold an idea of the distinctions of these styles." However, these distinctions have become blurred. "For example, you might see an Italian designer producing a very British-looking suit, or an American company designing suits with what was once considered a strictly Italian look," says Mr. Anderson.

•**American (or Sack or Ivy League):** The Sack suit, made popular in the early 1900s by Brooks Brothers and J. Press, is perhaps the archetypal American suit. It is distinguished by its boxy silhouette and *natural* (not padded or very lightly padded) shoulder. In its classic form, the Sack coat is *single-breasted* (a coat with a center closure secured with a single row of buttons). Sack coats typically have a single *vent* (the center slit in the back) and either two or three buttons. Trousers are not pleated and cut full.

The Sack Suit (single-breasted)

A variation on the Sack is the so-called *Updated American* suit, popularized by Paul Stuart in the middle of this century. The coat is slightly *suppressed* (tailored closely to the shape of the torso) and shoulders have more padding, imparting a slight "V-shape" to the torso. Trousers are often pleated and cut full.

•**British:** The British suit was created in London's Savile Row, home to generations of custom suitmakers, who have long been admired for their exquisite tailoring. There are some common touches among traditional Savile Row tailors, but no single style predominates. In general, the so-called "Savile Row" suit is more shaped than the American silhouettes. It has a tapered coat with particularly defined shoulders and high armholes.

Coats are either single-breasted or *double-breasted* (a coat that overlaps in front and has two rows of buttons) and commonly have a *ticket* (or "change") pocket and two high side vents, according to Steven Liao, owner of Gentle Custom Tailor, who has some 40 years' experience making suits.

Trousers generally have a high waist, two or three pleats on each side of the fly, and a generous cut.

Keep in mind, however, that Savile Row is now known more as a standard of tailoring excellence than as a suit style.

British Silhouette
(double-breasted)

•**Italian:** The Italian silhouette generally is regarded as sleek, modern and cutting-edge. Italian suits are often associated with the padded-shouldered but softly cut silhouette created by the designer Giorgio Armani in the 1970s. But Italian suits first came into their own in the 1950s, largely as a result of the popularity of the suits by Italian suitmaker Brioni.

Brioni's stylistic departure from American and British silhouettes was marked by a longer, tighter-fitting coat (often unvented), slightly accentuated shoulders and bolder colors and patterns. In general, Italian suits' lapel notches and buttons are slightly higher than those of American and British coats. Discreet, and therefore dressier, the *besom* pocket (a pocket without flaps) is common on Italian suit coats.

As with American and British suits, it would, however, be incorrect to pigeonhole the Italian silhouette. "There's no single Italian cut. In fact, there's a dramatic difference from city to city—from Naples to Rome to Torino," says Tom Kalenderian, executive vice president of men's merchandising at Barneys New York.

Italian Silhouette
(double-breasted)

8

Moreover, Italian suits often resemble Savile Row suits and American suits, although they usually add an elegant twist. "The Italians really mimic a great deal of what Saville Row does, but they look to sort of spin it to a much finer taste level, in terms of what they do with their fabrics and combinations," says Daniel Patrick Heaney, general manager of Sulka.

How can I know which of these suit styles is best for me?

Suit silhouettes convey very different "statements." Generally, suits that are tailored more closely to the shape of a man's physique are

---

WHAT THE EXPERTS SAY ABOUT CLASSIC SUIT STYLES

The Sack suit is a Brooks Brothers classic. We've found that there's a certain customer who buys it, and he is classic American. But even classics which have been around for forty years don't go untouched, and we make small changes to keep them modern.

—Jarlath Mellett, executive vice president and design director, Brooks Brothers

We've seen the industry shift toward the Anglo-American aesthetic. Other designers these days are going back to basics, back to the traditional look—more traditional silhouettes and fabrications and colors. It's a reawakening for them, while Paul Stuart has always offered more color and zest, typical of the British approach.

—Paul Stuart spokesman

In the mid-1950s, the concept of men's fashion was virtually non-existent. Brioni made a statement by offering a new attitude toward elegance, and helped create what is now known as the Italian style. We made a significant impact by offering unique fabrics, for example woven silks in brilliant colors, while maintaining all the characteristics of a traditional, custom-made suit. Our silhouette was closer to the body, with a higher button stance and armhole; the shoulder was slightly built up. Because of our revolutionary product with a fit that complemented men, the Hollywood of the 1950s discovered and embraced Brioni, with stars like Clark Gable, Gary Cooper, Henry Fonda and Cary Grant wearing our clothes. That tradition continues today.

—Joseph Barrato, CEO, Brioni America

---

dressier and, to some, appear more showy than do suits with boxy or "drapey" sihouettes.

Colors, patterns and fabrics also send signals about the man who wears them. Bold shades and patterns are attention-grabbing, while dark solids and subtle patterns impart a subdued look. Suit fabrics also tell people how formal you mean to be: cotton and linen, for example, are a bit less formal than worsted wool.

So, which is the right suit style for you? The answer depends on a number of factors: your profession, your physical appearance, your personality and your budget. The suit style you choose should harmonize with them all. Depending on your profession, you may need only one suit, perhaps slick and casual, for only occasional use. Or, you may need a dozen sober, traditional suits. The most important thing is to wear the best suit for you, not the suit that is being pushed as the latest trend.

Remember, you want to create your signature style, so you must determine if a certain suit really reflects who you are. Perhaps a sleek Italian suit would match your personality and body type better than a Sack suit would. You might find that a Savile Row expresses your personality perfectly. Also consider where you will be wearing the suit. Maybe a double-breasted Savile Row will look out of place at a casual office—which will make both you and your co-workers uncomfortable. If you aren't sure which suit style is best for you, ask a trusted salesperson or tailor.

Is there a difference between single- and double-breasted suits, apart from the fact that they button differently?

The double-breasted coat goes back as far the single-breasted does, in one variation or another, but the modern version is a Savile Row invention of the 1930s.

Single- and double-breasted suits express distinct attitudes. Double-breasted suits are considered dressier than single-breasteds because of their sharper lines, broad, padded shoulders, tapered sides and *peaked* lapels (lapels with pronounced lower points, reminiscent of lapels on some formalwear). Single-breasteds, which typically have *notched* lapels (lapels with points of equal width), are generally more subdued.

Double-breasteds never have vests; a vest would be concealed by the front fabric of the jacket. Double-breasteds are either not vented or have two side vents, which are dressier than the single vent that characterizes many American single-breasteds.

Because a double-breasted is arguably showier than the single-breasted, it may be a bit less versatile. For example, shirts with button-down collars are considered too casual for wear with a double-breasted. Further,

Peaked Lapel   *Notched Lapel*

some (though not all) experts say a double-breasted won't flatter a large man. If you don't like the look and feel of the double-breasted suit, however, you will appear awkward and self-conscious and, therefore, far from elegant.

Because the double-breasted suit coat has more fabric in front than a single-breasted, it always should be kept buttoned to prevent that fabric from gaping open. Of course, both single- and double-breasteds should be unbuttoned when you sit.

How many buttons should a suit have?

Although there is no correct number of buttons for a suit, most single-breasted suit coats through the decades have had two or three buttons. Therefore, for most men, two or three buttons is a good number.

Three buttons are traditional on Sack suits, the middle button of which is meant to be secured. Two buttons are typical on the Updated American suit, with the top button secured. Four buttons on a single-breasted are periodically trendy, yet at the same time they are anachronistic; they are actually circa 1895 fashion. "They're a costume," says custom suitmaker Jon Green of Jon

Green New York. On a four-button coat, all four buttons are fastened. One-button suits, popularized in France and the rave in the 1960s, are still worn, but are no longer common. Some say they impart a dandyish look, others say a simple elegance.

Double-breasted coats have four or six buttons, and either the middle or lower button should be secured.

Suit-coat sleeves usually have four buttons at the cuff but two or three are not heretical. They should be just nudging one another, which creates a finer appearance than buttons that are spaced apart. Some designers, moreover, prefer sleeve buttons that slightly overlap in a scalloped sequence.

Sleeve buttons originally served a function, allowing men to roll up their suit-coat sleeves when necessary. These days, working sleeve buttons are found only on custom-made suits or the finest ready-mades, and so may indicate fine craftsmanship in other areas of the suit.

What are the classic fabric patterns for suits? And are some dressier than others?

Suits of solid dark gray or navy blue are considered the most conservative. But suits with patterns can be extremely dressy and elegant, especially those bearing classic patterns, such as pinstripe, chalk stripe, Glen plaid, herringbone, houndstooth, window pane, nail head, sharkskin, crow's feet or bird's eye. There are also myriad other traditional plaids and checks.

As a rule, the subtler the patterns and the darker the colors, the dressier and more traditional-looking the suit will be. Pinstripes are among the most business-like and conservative of patterns, and they offer more personality than do the solids. Pinstripes are about 1/16 inch wide and are mostly muted white or blue, but can also be found in burgundy and other colors. Chalk stripes, a bit bolder and therefore a bit less dressy, are about 1/8 inch wide and are usually white.

Finally, checks and plaids tend to be somewhat busier, but a muted Glen plaid, for example, creates a conservative appearance.

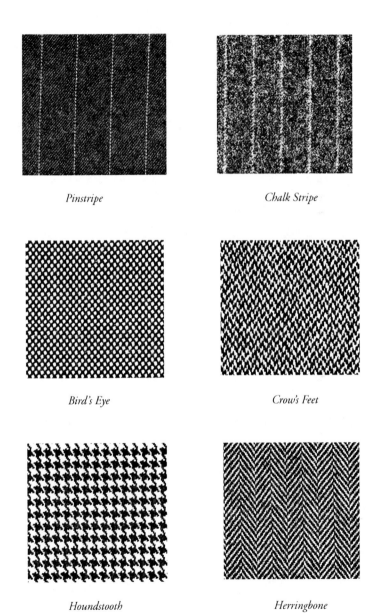

Pinstripe

Chalk Stripe

Bird's Eye

Crow's Feet

Houndstooth

Herringbone

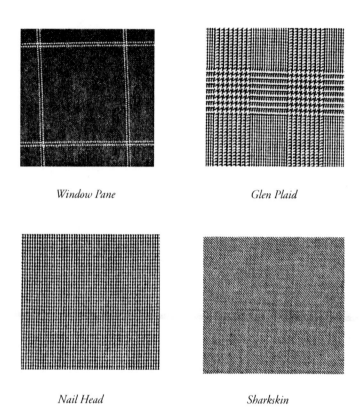

Window Pane

Glen Plaid

Nail Head

Sharkskin

Courtesy of Beckenstein Men's Fabrics

Three-piece suits seem a bit old-fashioned. Is there any reason I should wear one?

A *three-piece suit* (a suit with a vest) does impart a "buttoned-up" appearance and, some say, one that's old-fashioned. However, a vest does add refinement to a suit.

"To me, there's nothing dressier than a dark suit with a vest," says Alfred Arena, associate chairperson of the menswear design department at New York's Fashion Institute of Technology. And if you take off the coat, you'll still look smart. Of course, you can forego the vest and wear your suit as a two-piece.

WHICH SUIT STYLES ARE BEST FOR SUCCESS?

In this age of fast hiring and promoting, some managers are making decisions on people in the first ten seconds of a meeting. This decision can just as commonly be made at a brief encounter as at a cocktail party. And one's dress as well as social graces often figure as a potent factor in making an overall appraisal of one's suitability for a position. Sometimes it takes only one item out of place to be seriously questioned as to whether you can dress well. When you dress appropriately, others know that you know the rules, that you're playing by them very well and that you're all business. You want to respect those around you and be respected; dressing well has more to do with that than most people realize. Sometimes I cringe when I hear a story of how a promotion was denied because of a man's failure to know how to dress properly. Management responds by assuming that if he can't dress well, he may not be able to adapt to what is necessary in other parts of a job.

Generally, the darker the suit, the stronger the image projected. But there are exceptions in certain industries and climates. Fellows in their twenties and thirties in conservative fields most likely should think more seriously about sending a signal of all-business, not trendy. Stick with a two- or three-button suit in dark tones—blue, dark gray or black.

Notice what your boss or department head is wearing, and try to see if he is well-respected in how he dresses. Position yourself. You can dress like your boss, but if you dress better than he, it might be dangerous. If you know your boss is going nowhere in the company, there must be reasons, and perhaps one of those reasons is that he doesn't look the part and has refused to make efforts to change that. In that case, dress like other people who are clearly moving up and look sharp.

—*Frederick Knapp, image consultant, Frederick Knapp Associates Inc.*

Which is preferable on a coat—a single vent, double vents or no vents?

All three are equally acceptable, but they are not all acceptable on all suit styles. The single-vent suit (a British invention) evolved from the equestrian coat, which had a vent so that the tail of the coat would part at the saddle, and the vent retains this sporty air.

Double vents (also British) are said by some to be more elegant, because they drape more gracefully and maintain the suit's silhouette better than the single vent.

The ventless jacket (a European innovation) is arguably the dressiest of the three because of its smooth appearance. Therefore, the ventless style is a bit out of place on the countrified tweed jacket, which is better served by a single vent. The dressy double-breasted suit properly has two vents or none, but not one.

I've heard that brown suits are inappropriate for business attire. Is this true?

For decades it's been widely maintained that brown suits are not right for businesswear, although many have disagreed. Browns—particularly warm, dark browns—have long been thought of as colors of the outdoors. "Brown is a color traditionally associated with the country," explains suitmaker Mr. Green. These associations linger, despite the loosening of customs in America about business attire. A brown suit should be bought with this in mind.

I see black suits and white suits worn by celebrities but not by my colleagues. Are these colors special?

Black suits were worn in the sober Victorian era, but are hardly worn at all today, except by a few men attuned to trends. Now, black suits are seen as stark, and perhaps suggest mourning, rather than sobriety.

White suits are dandyish, casual and redolent of the South in summer. So, yes, suits of black or white do differ from those of other colors, and a man should wear them only if he is supremely confident in the appropriateness of such a choice.

Which suits are classics and are cool in the summer?

Classic summer suits have the same silhouettes as suits for the other seasons, but both the colors and fabrics are generally lighter. Traditional summer fabrics are cotton (seersucker, poplin and gabardine) and linen—but linen wrinkles easily and is seldom worn for business. Single-breasted cotton suits of medium-hued blue or tan poplin never go out of style. You also can wear wool year-round. In summer, wear suits or jackets of *tropical* wool (tightly-woven, hard finished and light-weight worsted-wool fabric). Suits with partial linings or no linings are also excellent for summer.

What are the standard coat pocket styles?

As a general rule, the less conspicuous the pocket, the dressier the coat. Below are descriptions of standard coat pockets.

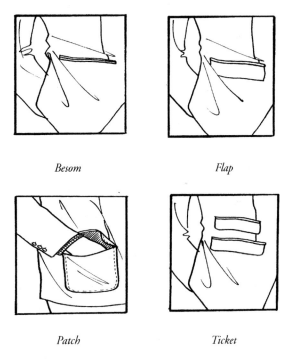

Besom   *Flap*

Patch   *Ticket*

•**Besom:** Used on tuxedo coats, the besom is a slit, formed by stitched folds on the top and bottom of the pocket opening. Besom pockets are often used on sleeker suit coats, and seldom on business suits.

•**Flap:** The flap is common on the two side pockets and on the ticket pocket.

•**Patch:** Flapped or unflapped, the patch pocket is constructed with exposed seams, which impart a casual look. Patch pockets are frequently used on tweed and camel hair sport jackets.

•**Ticket (or Change):** Often on British suits and sport jackets, the ticket pocket is a small flap pocket located above the side pocket. As its name suggests, it was meant for holding small items such as tickets or coins.

•**Chest:** The chest pocket (also known as a *welt* pocket), always located on the left breast, is often slanted upward toward the shoulder and is not flapped. It is used for holding a silk pocket square or a linen or cotton handkerchief.

I can afford to buy only a few good suits. Which styles would create a versatile core wardrobe?

Most men working in offices which require suits should own at least three, not only for variety, but also to allow the suits to rest between wearings.

The natural impulse might be to buy the suits that appeal to you the most. But retailers and tailors will tell you that a man should build a core suit wardrobe by selecting the most versatile styles. That means you should choose styles that have the longest staying power and those which work easily with the rest of your clothes and with your circumstances. An architect in Houston, for example, probably would start in a different direction than a young trader on Wall Street, for reasons dictated by the regions' climates, the working environment, and what clients and colleagues deem appropriate.

However, given these parameters, many experts suggest some variations on the classic conservative styles, colors and fabrics. For the traditional office, they recommend suits with dark, solid colors, such as navy-blue or gray, or subtle patterns, such as pinstripes. Single-breasteds are more versatile than double-breasteds, because they can be "dressed down" more easily.

Buying Your Suit

Suit prices range widely and are determined mainly by the quality of the fabric, the amount of handwork and, often, the name on the label. The following should demystify the process of judging a

---

The Core Suit Wardrobe

The first suit should be dark gray, which is good for the office and acceptable for social functions. Then, move on to a blue suit, which is a little more formal and better for weddings. After these basics, get one with a little more panache, like a Glen plaid. For more casual occasions, get a blue blazer and a tweed sport coat.

You've covered the basics so far, so your next suits should include more color or pattern. Then, after you have all this, get a suit with brown tones, which is stylish but not that flexible. Every well-dressed man should have both single- and double-breasted styles, and I typically don't recommend single vents. Remember, it's better to own a few well-made and versatile suits than a lot of poorly made ones.

—*Domenico Spano, designer and tailor, Bergdorf Goodman*

I would strongly recommend that the first suit for a man be a solid black or blue. These are so versatile one can use the coat as a blazer. The second suit should be light gray, with a little pattern, like window panes or plaids. Be elegantly creative with your shirts and ties. Stripes come later and have a nice slimming effect. Then look for a sport coat, which can be dressed up or down. Remember, there is more flexibility [in today's office dress codes], so having a number of different patterns, for example, is more acceptable. Confining oneself only to the classic business "uniform," popularized by the so-called IBM blue uniform, is really not appropriate these days. Today, there is more room for individuality and, in fact, IBM agrees on this.

—*Luciano Franzoni, designer and men's fashion analyst*

A young guy should start with items that don't fall out of fashion. Build a solid, traditional wardrobe first, then you can use additional accessories, or furnishings, like a different shirt or tie, to add to it. Stick with solids first. One can dress them up with more formal shirts and cuff links, or dress them down with a tattersall [shirt] and club tie.

—*Walter B.D. Hickey, Jr., chairman, Hickey-Freeman*

suit's quality and fair value. Remember the advice of Domenico Spano, designer and tailor at Bergdorf Goodman: "Great clothes elicit a comment like, 'Wow, you look great,' instead of, 'That must be an expensive suit you're wearing.'"

What are the differences among custom, made-to-measure and ready-to-wear suits?

Custom: A *custom* suit is hand-made to your specifications. It is also known as a *bespoke* suit because the suit's details are "spoken for" by the customer.

You may well spend many hours with the tailor during several visits. The paper pattern and, more important, every stitch are completely done by hand. Sleeves even have working buttonholes. A custom suit can cost triple the price of an expensive ready-to-wear suit and can take months to make, but a good one will last for a lifetime.

The grand tradition of custom tailoring was born in London's Savile Row, and a good custom Savile Row suit remains a model of fine workmanship. Well-made custom suits are meant to accommodate every contour of one's body, one's posture and the slightest physical irregularities.

Made-to-Measure: A *made-to-measure* suit is one for which you choose the style and fabric. The tailor sends your measurements to a shop or a factory, where adjustments are made to a pre-produced suit pattern. You may not find hand-sewn buttonholes and the like, but you will also not spend as much as you would on a custom suit. And you'll probably get thousands of fabrics to choose from and, presumably, a terrific fit.

Ready-to-Wear: A *ready-to-wear* suit is one that is sold completely finished (except for the trouser length). Some ready-to-wear suits have some handwork; others are made completely by machine. A ready-to-wear suit seldom fits a man as well as a custom or made-to-measure suit, even after it is significantly altered. That's because these suits are designed with leeway in the armholes and elsewhere, in order to accommodate the "average" build—which may not precisely match your proportions. So, have the best tailor you can find work on those areas which need altering. A good tailor will alter not only the coat sleeves and trouser buttons, but he will also adjust the seat, waist, collar, shoulders and chest.

THE ANATOMY OF A BESPOKE SUIT

We start with a two-hour consultation, for an important reason. We aim to design a suit that fits a man's life as naturally as it fits his body. So we talk about what he does for a living, as well as how he wears a suit. I inhabit the world of my clients and, therefore, I can help them feel more confident in deciding on style—how they will look and be received in a particular cut and color of suit.

How the man will wear a suit informs our choice of fabrics. We ask whether he is sitting at a desk all day and whether he keeps his jacket on or hangs it on the door. We ask him if he is getting in and out of the car often, or traveling frequently by train or by plane. Then we discuss the advantages and disadvantages of a range of possible fabrics, along with elements of style, such as buttons and pockets.

Next, measurements are taken and the fabric is ordered. In the meantime, we create a paper pattern, which is used as a template for the suit. Then we cut the fabric and begin constructing the suit in layers, starting with the hand-sewn canvas that forms the soul of the suit. The coatmaker sews the chest piece on top of the canvas, in order to shape the coat front to the man's body. Shoulder pads are added next, sewn into the lining by hand with silk thread.

Hundreds of stitches are made in the lapel and collar, so that these areas maintain their shape for the life of the suit. In fact, a master tailor can only make one and one-half coats a week. Not including the fitting, cutting and pattern-making, one coat requires approximately thirty hours of the tailor's dedication.

At the second fitting, our client tries on a sleeveless coat. Our focus is on precise markings at the chest, collar, waist and seat areas. When these alterations are made, a third, and usually final, fitting is done, where we finish the sleeves and make any final adjustments to the body of the suit.
—*Jon Green, suitmaker, Jon Green New York*

Are custom-made or made-to-measure suits worth the expense and time?

With completely hand-made suits starting at about $2,000, but averaging around $3,000, most men could never entertain the idea of buying one. Furthermore, a high-quality ready-to-wear suit should serve one's needs well.

A custom suit, however, may be a good option if you have a special size requirement or a job that demands an especially fine appearance. Most men who own a bespoke suit find wearing a machine-made suit dismaying. Moreover, makers of bespoke suits point out that the bespoke suit's durability and quality make it a sound investment. "We've worked on some suits which are fifty years old, and they still look impeccable," says Crittenden Rawlings, president and CEO of Oxxford Clothes, one of the largest and most important makers of hand-made suits in the United States. "The hand-made suit has a certain suppleness, which gives the garment a longer life. It conforms to the body and will retain fit, shape and expression for many years. This is not true of machine-made suits. Buying fine clothing makes a man feel positive about himself. Wearing a fine custom-made suit can be quite addictive."

Be warned, however, that there is such a thing as a poorly made custom suit, just as there are mediocre made-to-measure and ready-to-wear suits. "A very well made, machine-made suit is better than a bad hand-made suit," says Garrick Anderson, of Garrick Anderson Sartorial. "However, there is nothing like a fine, hand-made suit," he adds.

How can I recognize a well-made suit?

It's a lot more involved than merely looking at the price tag and brand label. In broad terms, look for signs of superior fabric and superior hand-tailoring.

When it comes to high quality, there is seldom a real bargain to be had: "If you want a good suit, you have to pay for it," says Christopher Pendleton, CEO of Aquascutum. Depending on the suit, you will be paying for the labor put into making it, the fabric

SUITS
30-SECOND QUALITY TEST

•**Fabric:** The fabric should drape naturally. Colors should be true, patterns defined. Should be made of fine yarns only (e.g., worsteds should approach cashmere in feel, and not be shiny; tweeds should be rich in color, and not stiff).

•**Stitching:** Stitching should be clean and strong. Hand-stitching, when used, is evident: where the lining is stitched to the coat; at the lapel edges; under the collar and lapel; at the buttonholes; at the trouser fly seam; inside the trouser waist; and at the belt loops.

•**Lapels:** Lapels should have a slight roll where they begin to fold back, and should not be stiff, flat, wrinkled or crimped.

•**Hand-Stitched Canvas:** The best coats are not fused.

•**Fully Lined Coat:** Made of fine rayon or silk, the lining should be well tailored, especially at hem, where lining is hung, folded and pressed.

•**Patterned Fabric:** Patterns should line up at the pockets and at the back of the collar.

•**Pocket Flaps:** Flaps should lie neat and flat.

•**Buttons:** Buttons should be made of natural horn, mother-of-pearl, polished brass or ceramic.

•**Suspender Buttons:** Buttons should be attached to the inside of the trouser waistline.

and buttons and, last but not least, the label. Of course, the craftsmanship and quality of the material and buttons are what you want to be paying for, not the label.

Some general rules of thumb are listed below. Keep in mind that only the finest bespoke suits will satisfy all the criteria.

•**Fabric:** A first impression of a suit's quality—as opposed to its style or fit—is based on the quality of the fabric (see section on fabrics later in this chapter). If the fabric is inferior, chances are that the rest of the suit will be, too. It takes only one touch to discern the quality of the fabric. High-quality worsted wool, of which most suits are made, has a smooth, supple *hand* (the feel of fabric, as determined by its weight and texture), which approaches even cashmere or silk; heavier wools, such as tweed, should be substantial but not stiff. Colors of all high-quality fabrics should look rich, well-defined and natural.

• **Stitching:** The stitching throughout should be clean and strong. All stitching in custom-made suits is done by hand. You can recognize hand-stitching because it is not perfectly measured. Any evidence of hand-stitching is a good sign. Hand-stitching maintains a suit's shape and allows give at points of stress better than machine-stitching does. Look for hand-sewn buttonholes; you can recognize them by stitching that is rough and uneven on the inside of the coat.

Also, examine where the lining is attached to the jacket for hand *felling* (wider stitches), which is a bit looser than machine felling. This will keep the lining from pulling if there is any shrinkage. Other places to look for hand-stitching include: lapel edges; under the collar and lapel; along the trouser fly seam; inside the waist of the trouser; and along the belt loops.

• **Lapels:** Lapels are perhaps the most conspicuous part of the suit, so they should be well made. They should be smooth; any wrinkling or crimping are signs of a poorly made suit. Lapels on bespoke jackets have a slight *roll* (a curving of the fabric). Many machine-made suits have lapels with no roll and look as flat and as stiff as cardboard—or, worse, the lapels actually curve outward from the chest.

• **Canvas:** If a suit is completely hand-made, a piece of canvas, or similar fabric, has been sewn into the chest area to help the jacket keep its shape and drape better. A suit with no canvas is termed "unconstructed." A sewn canvas hangs freely between the coat's outer and inner fabric. You can feel the canvas as a separate layer if you give the front of the coat a rub between your fingers. Most ready-to-wear suits are at least partly *fused* (glued) together. In a fused coat, the canvas is glued to the fabric, so that only two layers can be felt when rubbed. Hand-sewn canvases are becoming rare, because they are expensive to make. Keep in mind that while a hand-stitched canvas means the finest quality, fused suits have improved substantially in recent years. They are shedding their reputation for producing, over time, bubbles, creases and overall stiffness, caused by drycleaning, which can dissolve the fusing glue. Cheaper fusing methods, however, can produce a suit that will look shabby quickly. What you get with a hand-sewn canvas is a suit that will never suffer such aging problems.

"I'm not necessarily against the fused suit—I've seen some that are very impressive," says Richard Press, a former executive of J. Press, clothier to Frank Sinatra, Cary Grant and Robert Redford, among others. "But, then again, I've seen some that are simply grotesque—from famous designers—that aren't at all inexpensive."

•**Lining:** The coat should have a *lining* (an inner fabric) throughout the chest, back and sleeves. Good suits are lined with *bemberg* (a high-quality, lustrous type of rayon), unless it is tailored in the traditional German way, which excludes lining but not at the expense of quality. At the back of the coat, the lining should be loosely felled along the edges, and folded to form a crease, which hangs about a 1/4 inch above the coat's bottom edge.

•**Patterns:** Fabric patterns, such as stripes, should line up at all pockets, and where the back of the collar meets the back of the jacket. Some suit coats have patterns that also line up at the seams where the sleeves meet the shoulders.

•**Pockets:** Pockets should be smooth—no wrinkles, bunching.

•**Suspender Buttons:** Trousers should have buttons to allow you the option of wearing suspenders.

•**Buttons:** The finest suits have buttons made from natural horn (e.g., water buffalo or reindeer) or ground natural horn combined with a resin. Other top-quality buttons include those made from leather, mother-of-pearl, brass and ceramic. Joseph G. Barlow, president of clothier Harrison James, says a button is made of real mother-of-pearl if it feels cool to the touch of your nose. He adds that better buttons have "domed" backs, a detail which gives the button a lift from the fabric. Further down the quality scale are well-made plastic buttons, but, as Mr. Barlow says, "there really is no such thing as a great plastic button."

Also, determine whether buttons are sewn on by hand. Hand-sewn buttons are secured by threads sewn through the button-holes in two parallel lines. Machine-sewn buttons are secured by threads that form an "X". On the finest suits, even the buttons on the sleeves are sewn on by hand and are functional.

GETTING FITTED

Once you've chosen a particular suit, the next step is to have it properly fitted—that is, to have the suit altered to make it most comfortable and most flattering to your physique. Many men's clothing stores employ both a *fitter* (the person who takes the measurements) and *tailor* (the person who does the cutting and sewing according to the fitter's measurement marks, but who can do the fitting as well). Working with fitters and tailors involves many things: patience, a certain self-knowledge, a degree of knowledge of clothing and, above all, trust. The following explains what you should know before you get fitted to ensure that your suit looks elegant.

What sizes are suits made in?
When buying ready-to-wear suits, you should know your suit size in advance, to save time and avoid confusion. Coat sizes range from 36 to 60; trouser waist-sizes usually are 6 inches smaller than the coat size (known as a "6 inch drop"; men with big chests and narrow waists require a greater "drop").

Suits also are offered in Short, Regular, Long and Extra Long

YOUR TAILOR IS YOUR FRIEND

It's a little like going to the doctor. You have to trust the man and the establishment, and price should not be the principal motivating factor. Try to find a tailor with a good reputation and a reputable fitting department. Remember one thing: you should not bark orders at a fitter. The best thing you can do is to politely tell him your wishes. But don't try to redesign the suit. If you don't trust him, then don't use him. But once you start, you must work with him, not against him. It does not serve any tailor worth his salt to let you leave his shop looking bad. Give him the credit he deserves—you'll demotivate him if you are demeaning and bossy. Treat him like the professional he is. That's when you really get results, and everyone is happy.

—*Domenico Spano, designer and tailor, Bergdorf Goodman*

for the majority of sizes. Most shops stock a wide selection of suits in the most common sizes, which range from 36 to 46, but don't offer as many suits sized 48 and larger, unless it's a store specializing in "big and tall" sizes.

Note that suit sizes vary somewhat among different manufacturers, so don't rely solely upon size; always try on the suit.

How can I be sure that my tailor knows what he's doing?

The best way to find out is to chat with your tailor. Ask him, respectfully, for his opinions on certain points of style that you already feel knowledgeable about. What does he recommend regarding trouser length? How much shirt collar should be exposed above the suit collar? And so forth. If you aren't satisfied, don't bring him your business. If you get reliable answers, you should still keep an eye on his chalk while he works. Have all alterations pinned in crucial areas of movement instead of merely chalked, so you can make sure, by feel as well as sight, that the planned adjustments are right.

After he's completed work on your suit, don't accept the result until you've tested it and are satisfied.

Make sure that the jacket covers your backside, that your torso is not being constrained, that the armholes are not too low. Also check that the suit collar sits well, that the trousers aren't too tight or too loose. A suit may feel great when you're being fitted, but might pull or look baggy during everyday wear. Check the areas that get the most wear and tear: seat, crotch, thighs, knees, waist and where the trouser creases break above the shoes. Do whatever you must to give these spots a workout. Walk up a flight of stairs two at a time; lift your arms straight in the air; bend down to tie your shoes. Sit down, cross your legs, move your arms as though you're giving a toast at a dinner party, etc.

Fabrics, including wool, can shrink when drycleaned. Ensure that the tailor accounts for this, or leaves ample material for letting out later—maybe you'll still have the suit in five years, when you're heavier. Go for at least two fittings, if necessary. Be as insistent on the second as on the first.

I know what I like when it comes to fit. How firmly should I insist on my preferences with my tailor?

If you don't have a trusted tailor or fitter, then you should find one before you're fitted for your next suit. Get acquainted with a salesperson whom you trust at one of the better men's shops, and chances are he will refer you to a good tailor. Once you find that tailor, the best rule of thumb is that if a man knows what he wants—and makes this known right off the bat—his tailor will most likely treat him with respect. A good tailor may politely try to steer you away from disastrous decisions but, in the end, the final decisions are yours, and it's his job to carry them out. A good tailor won't pressure you to make snap decisions, and you shouldn't concede to advice automatically, without reason. If you see eye-to-eye with your tailor, then you'll welcome—and even seek—his advice. You can show your appreciation for his fine work by returning with more of your business; it's not necessary to offer a tip.

How can I get the best possible fit?

When you get fitted for a suit, you should wear the same clothes and carry the same items that you normally do when you wear a suit: a dress shirt, undershirt, the right pair of underwear, cuff links (if you use them), tie, dress shoes, dress belt and wallet. Bring anything else you might routinely carry in your pockets—cigars, pen—whatever. If you wear your wallet in your front pocket, then make sure it's there during the fitting.

It's also important act naturally. If your posture is imperfect, then you should stand with imperfect posture. Always be fitted with multiple mirrors, so that you can easily see the work being done from all sides. You may notice something that the tailor doesn't. If you are in the least confused or bothered by the work, get an explanation from the tailor; this is the time to speak out, not after the real work is done.

What should I look for to determine whether my suit coat fits well?

Any creases or bulges tell you right away that the suit is ill-fitting. The suit coat should lie smoothly along the front and back when you are standing in a relaxed position. Horizontal creases between the shoulder blades indicate tightness in the shoulders; vertical creases in the middle of the back or under the arms tell you that the suit requires taking-in. When buttoned, the lowest button should be half-concealed by the front fabric of the jacket; if the button is completely exposed, the coat is too tight. Generally, a well-fitted suit moves *with* you, not *against* you. Some further guidelines include the following:

•**Coat Length:** The bottom of the coat is the vertical midpoint of the suit, and should be long enough to cover the seat of your pants. The waist button—the top button on a two-button jacket, and the middle button on a three-button jacket—should sit just below your natural waist. If the coat is too short, it won't drape properly; too long, and it will look overwhelming.

•**Sleeves:** The shirt's sleeve cuffs (assuming your shirt is well-fitted, with cuffs ending at your wristbone) should extend from your jacket sleeve by about 1/2 inch, so that the cuff shows. This is

especially important if you are wearing cuff links, which you want to be just partially revealed at the end of the suit sleeve. *This is a critically important detail*: if the shirt is not showing at all, there are serious problems with either the shirt or the coat, or both.

• **Collar:** The back of the coat collar should rest about 1/2 inch below the back of the shirt collar. If the coat bulges at the back of the neck, the collar should be altered so that it lies smoothly on the nape of your neck.

• **Lapels:** Lapels should not buckle outward when the jacket is buttoned. If they do, the jacket is too tight in the chest. Generally, lapels ought to extend no more than halfway to the shoulder (very narrow lapels go in and out of style, but they break the visual balance created by a proper lapel width).

• **Shoulders:** Accentuated suit shoulders, like lapel widths, go in and out of style, so it's best to stay with shoulders that comfortably agree with the size and shape of your own. Suit shoulders cut too broadly or too narrowly can throw off the proportion of your head and your height to your shoulders. However, if you have unusually narrow shoulders or a sloping posture, heavily padded shoulders might be flattering, because they'll keep the proportions of the suit intact.

• **Armholes:** Make sure the armholes are cut high enough. If they sit too low, they will cause the coat to lift at the slightest raising of an arm and ruin the appearance of the entire suit.

• **Vents:** A coat vent should lie flat. If a vent splays open, the coat is too tight.

How should a vest fit?

A vest should fit to ensure a well-tailored look with or without the jacket. Beware of a vest that is too tight, a common problem, which causes the shirt and tie to bulge. A loose vest will billow from your chest or creep up at the shoulders. The vest should lie smoothly in front and back, and should be long enough to conceal the trouser waistline and the bottom of the tie and, therefore, should reach the top of the trouser pleats. If the vest extends more than 2 inches below the waist, it is too long. The back lining is often made of the same fabric as the lining of the coat. Some vests have adjustable tabs in the rear but, even so, you will probably need the vest tailored. Note that the bottom button of a vest, by tradition, should not be fastened.

How should trousers fit?

You want your trousers to provide an elegant contour from your waist down to your shoes. Keep in mind the following points:

•**Waist:** Your trousers should be secured at the natural waist, or just below your navel. This may feel uncomfortable to those who grew up with hip-hugging jeans. But wearing suit trousers at the natural waist affords sufficient room in the crotch and thighs and allows the fabric to drape properly. Most suits are designed around this rule, so wearing your trousers too low can throw off proportions: vests won't fall where they should, your legs will appear shorter than they are, and your trousers may bunch at the ankles. For men who are uncomfortable with the belt at the natural waist, suspenders are a good alternative. Make sure that the waistband is loose enough so that you can sit without constriction.

•**Rise:** While your waistband should be at the waist, you want to be certain that your trousers provide you with ample room at the crotch and seat. The *rise* is the length from the bottom of the crotch to the waistband, and a low rise can be a permanent problem, causing tugging and pulling at the seat and thighs, and causing pockets to flare—problems difficult to solve. You want a generous rise, which ensures that your trousers can be worn comfortably at your natural waist. Horizontal creases around the fly, and pleats that splay out indicate that the trousers are too snug.

•**Length:** Your trousers should be long enough so that the *break* (the little buckling of the trouser's crease) is about 4 inches above the top of the shoe. A very deep break means your trousers are too long; they will look baggy and will distort the silhouette of the suit. A break that is too small means that your trousers are too short. Business suits usually have a medium break, which allows the trousers to cover socks, but without bagginess. Trouser bottoms should rest 1/2 inch above the top of the shoe's heel.

I never know what to answer when the tailor asks me if I want cuffs. Should I have my trousers cuffed?

Men did not commonly wear cuffs on trousers until about the turn of the century, when it became acceptable for men to roll up the bottoms of their trouser legs to prevent soiling. Tailors responded by adding the cuff to replicate that look. During World War II, cuffs were banned to save fabric, and the cuffless trouser came back into vogue and has remained with us to this day. There is no hard-and-fast rule regarding cuffs, but most tailors strongly recommend that trousers of business suits, particularly double-breasteds, have them. They create a dressier look, up to a point; tuxedos don't, or shouldn't, have them.

Cuffs serve several functions. They keep trousers anchored, which, in turn, allows pleats to drape properly and encourages the crease and the break. They also help keep your ankles covered when you walk. The traditional cuff width is 1 3/4 inches, but it may be wider or narrower for exceptionally tall or short men.

I've noticed that some trousers have pleats while others don't. Does it matter whether trousers are pleated?

Again, as with cuffs, there is no firm rule regarding pleats, except that they, too, make for a dressier look. Pleated trousers offer several advantages: they give you more room when you sit and walk. They also hide bulging if you keep articles in your pockets.

Two pleats are standard on each side of the fly seam—the longer pleat near the fly extends to the trouser crease; the shorter pleat extends to the bottom of the front side-pocket. Some trousers, however, have three pleats, or only one, on each side of the fly. Men with large girths might prefer trousers with pleats, because they are roomier than plain-front trousers and tend to hide unflattering weight. Plain-front trousers are generally preferred by conservative dressers.

Is it true that some suit styles are more flattering than others depending on a man's physique?

Yes, it is generally said that certain suit styles will make a man appear slimmer, larger, taller or shorter. Silhouettes and patterns that emphasize vertical lines tend to make one look taller; horizontal lines bring attention to one's girth. But don't feel compelled to follow these rules steadfastly. If you're tall and thin and prefer supple, lightweight wool pinstripes and feel comfortable with how you look, then wear them.

Which style of suit is best for very tall, slender men?

If you wish to de-accentuate your height, avoid stripes. Instead, opt for plaid, houndstooth or solid fabrics. Have the suit cut on the generous side with, perhaps, padded shoulders, flap pockets, healthy pleats and heavy cuffs. Use medium or heavy fabrics and three-button coats, which have shorter lapels.

Which suit flatters a bulky figure?

If you are heavy or muscular, you'll want to accentuate your height, not your width. Vertical lines, such as stripes, will achieve this. Don't wear trousers cut on the short side; don't let them ride your hips. Use supple fabrics, which won't add girth. Stay clear of anything that will stress the horizontal, such as flap pockets, wide lapels and cuffs.

Which looks best on short, heavy men?

Figure-hugging styles will only make you look heavier. Avoid double-breasted coats, pocket flaps and single vents. Trousers should have a long rise, and the waist should sit at the natural waistline (a belt underneath a paunch only accentuates the weight and makes legs look shorter).

Which complements short, slender men?

Keep the coat somewhat short, which will help make your legs appear longer. More pronounced shoulders and chest are recommended for this body type. Choose patterns that stress vertical lines. Wear trousers somewhat high on the waist, and make sure they have a healthy break and shorter cuffs or no cuffs.

Which suits are best for athletic builds?

Men with athletic builds need to balance a full chest with a relatively small waist—which could require some heavy tailoring. The Sack suit, with its natural shoulders, flatters these builds. Two- or three-button, single-breasted coats are equally amenable to the athletic build and are favored over double-breasteds (so as not to look too bulky). Choose medium-weight fabrics over heavy ones to play down musculature. Trousers ought to have a generous rise and be worn high on the waist.

Fabrics

Why are most suits made of wool? And what should I know about other fabrics?

Wool is the traditional fabric for suits because it is durable, warm and holds the suit's shape well.

Wool weights for suits typically range from 7 (the lightest) to 15 (the heaviest) ounces per square yard. It's a good idea to have suits in a range of weights, which will provide an all-season wardrobe. But with more men spending less time outdoors, and with the prevalence of climate-control, heavy fabrics are less desirable than they once were. A good all-season weight is 10 to 12 ounces. Over the years, however, mills have developed a wide range of new fabrics. Fabrics are being woven to impart a thicker, more textured *nap* (texture) while maintaining a light feel. Wool has been refined in ever lighter, more durable, and more breatheable weights and weaves. In addition, many mills have developed shrink- and wrinkle-resistant fabrics, some adding synthetic fibers to do so. Therefore, pay as much attention to the nap of the cloth as you do to its weight.

You may notice that some suits are made of "Super" wools. The term is a trade name that describes fabrics made of *merino* wool (wool of exceptionally fine fibers, named after the merino

THE "SUPERS": A BRIEF INTRODUCTION

Neal Boyarsky, "Fabric Czar," owner and president of New York's Beckenstein Men's Fabrics, sells fabrics to Hollywood tailors of film stars, including Tom Cruise and Al Pacino, and to scores of corporate titans. Mr. Boyarsky explains the differences among Super wools:

70s-80s: Classic, hard finish and very durable for everyday wear and good for all weather; fine for people who travel and sit a lot, because it wrinkles less than the finer fabrics.

90s-110s: These are fine for most businessmen, and are widely used in fine ready-to-wear suits. You have to be an expert to tell the difference between the 100s and 110s. But these are appropriate for an executive.

120s: Not for a guy who sits in the chair all day—he'll kill the fibers. Great for an important meeting, public or television appearances, for example.

150s and 180s: The cloth of princes, heads of state, and Forbes 500 executives. This is extremely costly, and reserved for suits that must be extra-fine, supple and not worn too much. The fiber is barely seen by the naked eye.

sheep). Super wool fabrics are classified in grades determined by the diameter (in microns) of the wool fibers. These grades were developed in units of 10, to create a simple, international standard of measurement. Simply put, higher grade wool is woven of thinner fibers than are lower grades. The classic 1950s suit fabrics, for example, were mostly 70s and 80s—fibers of thicker diameter than the finer fibers available today. "Super 100s" are at most 18.5 microns in diameter (but note that the "100" has no direct connection to the "18.5"). Now there are even Super 180s, which use fibers of 13.8 microns, which are barely visible. Generally, the fineness of the fiber is what dictates the expense of a fabric. "You're seeing a lot more luxurious fabrics—Super 100s and 120s, 150s—and that's the one common thread among all the basic silhouettes," says Paul Stuart. "Everyone is going to finer, lighter weight suits for all-weather."

Below are some of the more common fabrics you'll find when browsing through suit racks or flipping through swatch books.

Worsted Wool: Worsteds are a broad family of fabrics made from long-staple fibers commonly woven to impart a hard *finish* (surface texture). Worsteds make great suit material because they are durable, yet breathable. Worsted wools differ from *woolens*, which are loosely woven fabrics that have a soft, textured feel.

•**Cheviot:** Named after the type of sheep this wool is taken from, Cheviot is known for its heavy-duty, burly nap.

•**Corduroy:** Usually made of cotton, this fabric comes in wide or narrow *wale* (the velvet-like rib), with the latter considered dressier.

•**Crepe:** A light, spongy fabric, usually of silk or rayon. Used for somewhat casual suits.

•**Flannel:** Wool flannel is loosely knit and imparts an elegant, draped effect when used in a suit. The gray flannel suit is a classic example of a woolen. Flannel is usually made in heavier weights.

•**Gabardine:** A twill of cotton or wool that is woven tightly in order to produce an extremely durable fabric that holds a crease exceedingly well.

•**Linen:** Made of flaxen fibers, linen wrinkles easily. It is sometimes used to make suits.

•**Moleskin:** A thick, cotton fabric with a chamois-like nap. Extremely durable, and usually used for hunting and fishing, or general outdoor wear.

•**Poplin:** A tightly woven, lightweight fabric, usually cotton.

•**Seersucker:** Generally made of cotton, seersucker is woven to impart its signature crinkled texture. It has puckered white stripes alternating with stripes of blue, green, pink or yellow. Seersucker is commonly used for summer suits, sport jackets and trousers.

•**Sharkskin:** Sharkskin is a type of worsted wool. It's woven with two shades of yarn in a twill weave to produce a hard-finished fabric, usually with barely distinguishable lighter tones on a darker background.

•**Tweed:** Tweed is known for its nubby textures and variegated earthy tones. Commonly used for cold-weather sport jackets and overcoats, tweeds are also sometimes used for suits. The most well-known tweeds are: *Harris* (the heaviest tweed, known for warm colors in herringbone patterns); *Shetland* (from the Shetland Islands of Scotland, typically in plaids and stripes, and generally a lighter weighted weave); and *Donegal* (typified by flecks of color, such as blue, red and yellow, throughout the fabric).

•**Twill:** Any fabric, but usually one of cotton or wool, that possesses a twill weave—a weave that has raised ribs on the diagonal. A twill is a broad, blanket term for fabrics, from khaki to Super 180s wools. Cavalry twill is especially heavy.

There are a lot of synthetic blends out there. Should I give them a try, or are they a sign of an inferior suit?
Synthetics, such as rayon, nylon and polyester, have been used in suits for decades. Purists may abhor any unnatural fabric, but certain synthetics have earned the status of a classic. Some suits are made with synthetic stretch fibers, for greater comfort. Synthetic fibers also resist wrinkling, and can be lighter in weight than natural fibers. The downside of synthetics is that they can age poorly. You may encounter fibers with names like elastane, lycra and polyamide. A good bet is to try these in blends containing low percentages combined with wool or other natural fibers. Perhaps you'll prefer the lighter feel and weight to pure wool.

Caring for your suit

How do I keep my suit looking great?
The following pointers will prolong the life of your suits:

•**Rest:** Avoid wearing the same suit on consecutive days, which may distress the fabric, because it won't have time to air out or return to its proper shape.

•**Brush:** Give the suit a quick brushing with a soft-thistled brush to remove dust and particulate matter from smog.

•**Hang Properly:** Before hanging up your suit, empty the pockets of items that may cause wrinkling or bunching; zip up trousers; and fasten buttons. Hang suit coats on substantial, wooden hangers, and hang the trousers upside-down by the cuffs on a clamp hanger. Draping trousers over a hanger may cause unwanted creases.

•Give your suits adequate space in the closet; ensure that they aren't touching other clothes. This lets the fabric breathe.

•Place cedar chips or a few moth balls in a box on the floor of your closet to repel moths.

•If the suit is wrinkled, try hanging it in the bathroom with steam from the shower. Then let it air out.

•Avoid drycleaning your suit too often. There's usually no need to dryclean a suit more than once every five times you wear it; some experts suggest drycleaning once every ten or 12 wearings. It is often sufficient to get your suit steam-pressed to remove wrinkles and refresh trouser creases, instead of having it drycleaned. Never iron a suit because the hot metal might damage the material. Summer suits of cotton or linen, which tend to absorb perspiration, may need more frequent cleaning.

•If storing a suit for a long period, seal it in a plastic garment bag.

DRESS
SHIRTS

Attire speaks before you have the chance to utter your first word.

— Alexander S. Kabbaz, custom shirtmaker

Style is knowing what you can wear, what you can pull off, what looks really good on you. And adding your own twist to pull it all together.

—Karen Albano, sales associate, Robert Talbott

A shirt with a crisp, well-shaped collar, impeccable cuffs and luxurious cotton shows the world that your good taste doesn't end with your suit. Fine shirting fabric will be admired by colleagues when you remove that jacket and roll up your sleeves. And those fabrics no longer must be solid white or blue. Most companies have abandoned that dreary white-or-blue-only shirt policy. Follow the lead of London's famed Jermyn Street shirtmakers, who disproved early and with ingenuity the notion that a dress shirt must be dull. Shirts can provide your suit and tie with a backdrop of lush colors and striking designs: turquoise chalk stripes, russet-and-gold checks, tan-and-maroon tattersall and an infinite variety of others. However, there's more to building a shirt wardrobe than collecting a bunch of costly, colorful cotton miracles of shirtmaking. We explain, below, how to select your shirts knowledgeably.

What are the most important things I should consider when buying a dress shirt?

When you're choosing a shirt, pay special attention to the two most noticed features: the shape and size of the collar, and the quality of the cotton.

Many shirtmakers, such as Mark Sahmanian, president of Paris Custom Shirt Makers, Inc., believe that the collar's shape is more important than the shirting fabric's quality. "Fabric is important but not as important as the collar, because when people are talking to you, they are looking at your face, so they see the collar more than the fabric," says Mr. Sahmanian, who through 49 years as a custom shirtmaker has made shirts for men such as Britain's Prince Charles and President Ronald Reagan. He adds: "The cuff is also important because the cuff shows from your jacket sleeve."

Most men ought to follow this simple rule for collars: avoid extreme dimensions. Your collar should flatter the shape of your face and the length of your neck, and a collar of medium proportions will probably suffice. So keep your collar *points* (the collar tips) about 3 inches long, and keep the width of the *spread* (the space between the collar's points, where the tie sits) from being too narrow or too wide.

However, if your face is exceptionally long or round, you may want a collar that provides counterbalance. A long face is best framed by a wide-spread collar with shorter points; a round face by a narrow-spread collar with somewhat longish points.

Your collar also should counterbalance the length or shortness of your neck: A long neck? Buy a higher collar. A short neck? Buy a shorter collar. "There is only one rule," says custom shirtmaker Alexander S. Kabbaz: "You don't put a fat, round face with a double chin and short neck on top of a wide spread collar."

Robert Gillotte, bespoke manager for Jermyn Street's Turnbull & Asser, agrees: "What's inappropriate is if the collar doesn't fit the wearer's face dimensions. It's really about the balance, about how it frames the face. Our endeavor is to always keep everything in balance."

Note, however, that as the spread of the collar points widens, the shirt's appearance becomes dressier (and your collar's spread, of course, should echo the formality of the rest of your attire). So, the trick is to balance tradition—and its dictates about how dressy a collar's width is considered to be—with how well it will complement your face.

The quality of the cotton is of critical importance, too, and will be explained in detail later in this chapter.

What are the classic collars?

•**Oxford Button-down:** The oxford button-down was brought to the United States from England in 1896 by John Brooks, grandson of the founder of Brooks Brothers, who observed that polo players wore collars with buttons to prevent the collar points from being blown in their faces. Because this collar's origin derives from sport, it appropriately is attached to a shirt of oxford cotton, a somewhat coarse, and therefore more casual, weave. Properly worn, this collar  should have a roll to it, rather than a flat foldover of fabric. To this day, it remains the most casual of all collar styles because of its unstarched appearance and its collar buttons (simplicity is the mark of dressiness in all men's clothing. Buttons work against this principle). "They're sloppy," says Mr. Kabbaz. "If I had to select two words and put them with button-down, they would be 'informal' and 'academic.'"

So wear a button-down with your sportier jackets (although in New England it is common for men to wear button-downs with even the dressiest suits). And it needn't be worn with a tie.

•**Straight (or Point):** The straight collar is dressier than the button-down, because it has no buttons and is stiffer.

Perhaps the most common and most versatile collar, it appears equally proper with suits, sport jackets or cardigans, and won't look amiss without a tie.

•**Spread:** The points of the spread collar are, as its name suggests, a bit wider apart than those of the straight collar; therefore, it is  considered dressier.

Wear this one with a tie, to fill the larger gap between the collar points. You may even want to wear a spread collar with a half- or full-Windsor tie-knot (see Neckwear chapter) in order to fill that empty space between the points.

•**British Spread:** The widest collar and arguably the dressiest of all. The large, empty area between the points demands that it be accompanied by a tie. Indeed, it can even comfortably accomodate the bulky Windsor knot. Men with round faces may want to avoid this collar in favor of the narrower spread collar.

• **Tab:** This tidy, some might even say constrained-looking, collar can nevertheless be flattering, especially on men with narrow or square faces (round-faced men may appear to be a bit choked). The collar—introduced to America by the Duke of Windsor—gets

its name for a snap (called a *tab)* that connects the collar points behind the knot of the tie. Usually used with a semi-spread collar, tabs are neater but not necessarily dressier than a non-tab semi-spread. "The tab collar is a nattier look," says Mr. Heaney of Sulka. "It performs the same function as a collar bar [a pin that pulls together the collar points] without the flashiness or showiness of that extra piece of jewelry. It pulls the collar under and into the knot so that your tie is more crisp and clean and prominently knotted."

• **White Contrast:** A white collar (usually paired with white French cuffs), so named because it contrasts with the patterned or colored fabric of the shirt's body and sleeves. Some say a contrast collar dresses up a shirt.

•**Band:** This really is not a collar at all, but a band of fabric where a collar would meet the body of the shirt. Today, band collars are worn not only for casual but also for formal affairs. But that's hardly traditional, according to Gregory deVaney, CEO of Turnbull & Asser: "That's a trend. It's fashion thing," he says. In other words, this collar is best reserved for casualwear.

Why should my dress shirts be made of fine cotton?
You want fine cotton because it not only looks dressier than coarser cotton weaves and other fabrics, but it also feels most comfortable against your skin. Silk shirts are rarely worn in most professions. Linen shirts are strictly for summer casual wear. Yes, pure cotton wrinkles more than when blended with artificial fibers, but its appearance is lusher and it holds color dyes faster.

How do cotton fabrics differ?
Not all cotton is alike. Just as collar style determines how dressy the shirt appears, so does the quality of the cotton: the finer the cotton, the dressier the shirt. And the longer the fiber, the finer the cotton, because there are fewer knots binding the fibers together. The longest cotton fibers are about 1 1/2 to 2 inches.

The best cotton is known as *Sea Island*, named for the island off Georgia's coast where this cotton was once grown. Today, Sea Island cotton seeds have been exported throughout the world, so Sea Island refers to the type of cotton, not where it is grown. *Egyptian* cotton, which is often grown from Sea Island seeds, is also among the highest quality. Another fine cotton is *Pima*, which is grown in America's southwestern states.

But not only is cotton of differing quality, it is also woven in different degrees of fineness, with the closer weaves and finer yarns providing a dressier shirt. *Two-ply* cotton—cotton made of two lengths of yarn intertwined—looks superior to single-ply cotton because its density adds lushness: "Two-ply is stronger and more elegant because it's thicker," says Mr. Sahmanian.

Broadcloth shirting fabric (synonymous with *poplin* shirting fabric) is made from fine yarns in a tight, plain weave that creates an almost silky appearance and is used for the dressiest shirts.

Another fabric used for fine dress shirts is *royal oxford,* which is woven diagonally—instead of at right angles—and has a silky hand. *Pinpoint oxford* is a broadcloth fabric woven with yarns thicker than plain broadcloth and so imparts a coarser nap. Pinpoint oxford is often used for more casual button-down collar shirts.

There is also *end-and-end* weave (also called *end-on-end*), which is essentially any weave—including those described above—that intertwines a white yarn with a colored yarn, which imparts a slightly checked pattern.

The best shirting fabrics are woven by mills in Italy, England and France.

Cotton may look good, but it wrinkles. I prefer the convenience and the smooth look of polyester blends. Is it a mistake to wear them?

Polyester spares you a wrinkled shirt but, on the other hand, convenience isn't everything, as purists argue. Cotton blended with polyester makes for a shirt that breathes less and lacks the vivid colors and the fine feel of a pure cotton shirt. Synthetic blends also don't age as well as pure cotton. However, blends do offer the benefit of easy care, particularly helpful if you travel a lot. But buy blends with more than 50 percent cotton, which provide the benefits of both pure cotton and synthetics.

Are striped and patterned shirts still considered more casual than those of solid colors?

The solid-white shirt remains the classic shirt for formalwear. But it is no longer the only shirt worn for business. Shirts of other solid colors, such as French blue, and patterns, such as pinstripes, are about as dressy as white and are often worn with business suits. But don't stray too far afield: solids of canary yellow or bottle-green and other off-beat hues are not as traditionally dressy as white solids and blue solids. And as the stripes—or checks or other patterns—grow bolder, the shirt grows more casual. And some bold patterns—tattersalls, checks, plaids—usually are best for casualwear.

47

How many dress shirts, and what styles, should I own for a core wardrobe?

If you work in an office that requires you to wear a suit or a jacket and tie, then you should own at least ten dress shirts, and it wouldn't hurt to have 12 shirts in your closet. Ten shirts should be sufficient to get you through the five-day work-week, plus provide you with a few extra shirts, either to add variety to your wardrobe or to compensate for mishaps, such as stains or loose buttons, which can put a shirt out of commission.

With less than ten shirts, you may not have enough shirts, or an adequate choice of shirts, to wear after you have sent some to be laundered.

Shirts of a solid white or blue should make up a substantial portion of your core shirt wardrobe, because they pair well with most ties and suits, and they are traditional shirt colors.

Other versatile shirts are those with subtle patterns, such as pinstripes, in adaptable colors, such as red, gray or blue.

THE CORE SHIRT COLLECTION

You should own a minimum of ten shirts, to rotate through the laundry. Two basic whites; two basic blues; a basic blue end-on-end; a classic blue-and-white stripe or wine-and-white stripe; maybe some tattersalls or checks.

—*Daniel Patrick Heaney, general manager, Sulka*

Most of your dress shirts should be made of broadcloth cotton, although you may want to have a few shirts with button-down collars and slightly coarser, more casual, cotton weaves, such as oxford. More casual shirts will allow you to dress down a suit or a sport jacket and, therefore, will provide some variety.

Shirts of less common colors, such as pastels, or those that have busy patterns, such as tattersalls, are not especially versatile, but can serve as a strong background player in your wardrobe.

Generally, a core shirt wardrobe should allow you to move stylishly from a casual sport jacket to a dressy suit.

How should a shirt properly fit?

Shirts usually are offered folded, pinned and wrapped in plastic. And most stores won't allow you to try on a shirt, because they are difficult to repackage. (Some better men's stores may allow you to try on a shirt, if you ask. If they won't, then ask a salesperson to help you choose the proper shirt.) So buying packaged shirts are a shot in the dark as far as fit is concerned. To increase the likelihood that you'll select a well-fitting shirt, you should know your collar size and sleeve length before you shop.

Collar sizes run by the half-inch (e.g., 14, 14 1/2, 15); sleeve lengths run by the inch (e.g., 30, 31, 32). Shirtmakers commonly make shirts that have two sleeve lengths per collar size, to accommodate a greater range of men (e.g., 14-32/33). This practice often makes the shirt sleeve either a bit blousy or a bit short. As a rule, it's better to select sleeves on the long side, because shirts shrink during the first three washes. (Of course, if you're buying shirts that are sized Small, Medium, Large, Extra Large, then getting the right fit is even more hit-or-miss.) It may be helpful to stay with one brand that fits you well, because shirt sizes are not perfectly standardized.

Historically, American shirts were cut fullest, French shirts were the most tapered, and English shirts fell somewhere in between, according to Mr. deVaney of Turnbull & Asser—although it's arguable how true this remains today. Mr. Heaney says that all three cuts are equally proper: "That's personal preference. Some men like a very full shirt because it's more comfortable. Others want a tapered shirt, because they want to look skinny. My experience has been that tapered shirts are not as comfortable and they don't stay tucked in as well." Take your pick. But if you tend to wear fitted suits, you may want to wear tapered shirts. If the armholes are too low and blousy—as they sometimes are on full-cut shirts—they may bunch up at your suit coat's armholes, which might make the sleeves ride up and look shorter than they should.

• **Sleeve Length:** Sleeve length should be measured from the center of the back of your collar, to one inch below your wrist bone, according to Mr. Sahmanian, of Paris Custom Shirt Makers. The tape runs along the top of your shoulder and along your arm, which should be slightly bent, to the wristbone. Add an inch to the tape number because the sleeve should be a bit long to allow for movement. But the cuff should be snug enough to keep it at the wrist. Most men's sleeve lengths fall between 32 and 36 inches.

• **Collar Size:** Collar size is determined by measuring around your neck just below your Adam's apple. If your collar size falls between half-inches, the larger measure is best to compensate for shrinkage. A collar that chokes will eventually be unbuttoned for relief, ruining your appearance; a collar also shouldn't be too loose. The right size means one-half size larger than your neck because cotton shrinks. If you can't slip two fingers between your collar and your neck, your collar is too tight. Sulka's Mr. Heaney says that two fingers should fit in the collar "because most better shirts are cut to allow for a half-inch of shrinkage in the collar. So when you get the shirt, the collar is always going to be a little loose until after the third washing. You wash it three times, and that's when it's shrunk to its maximum."

• **Shirt-tail Length:** Your shirt-tail hem should reach to your crotch, or it may pull free from your trousers when you sit or bend over.

I wear short-sleeved shirts under my suits and sport jackets in warm weather. I've been told it looks slovenly. Is it?

Not only is it *not* acceptable to wear short-sleeved dress shirts in the summer, it is not acceptable to wear such shirts in *any* season. This is because your sleeve cuff doesn't show beyond your jacket sleeve, and when you take off that jacket, your bare arms are exposed. The more bare skin that shows, the less dressy the look.

Should a dress shirt have a pocket?

Go back far enough and you'll find that all dress shirts were once made without pockets. Simplicity has been the key element of dressy attire since at least the 19th century. Even today, custom shirtmakers won't attach a pocket unless you ask them to. "There is a place for a pen," says Turnbull & Asser's Mr. deVaney, "And it's in a desk or in your jacket pocket." Mr. Kabbaz says he sews pockets on shirts "only if I lose the argument."

Today, ready-made dress shirts have one pocket or no pocket. If a shirt has two pockets, it's not a dress shirt. As for monograms, keep them discreet, and where the pocket would be.

When should I wear shirts that have French cuffs?

French cuffs (foldover cuffs with holes for cufflinks) should be worn when, and *only* when, you wear cuff links to fasten the cuff. Cuff links are worn with formalwear and businesswear. Otherwise, wear shirts with *barrel cuffs* (cuffs secured with one or more buttons).

How can I recognize a well-made shirt?

•**Fabric:** The most important thing to look for in a shirt is the quality of the cotton. Ignore labels and just run your fingers over it. The better the cotton, the softer it will feel. The best cotton, Sea Island, feels similar to silk. Colors will be defined and brighter on high-quality cotton.

•**Single-Needle Seams:** This means the seam is sewn along one side, then on the reverse by the same needle, rather than sewn by two needles side-by-side. Single-needle stitching provides a cleaner look because seams sewn by double needles tend to bunch up (as seams do on denim pants).

•**Stitching:** Make sure there are no loose threads on the seams, buttons or buttonholes.

•**Pleats:** Better shirts have pleats in the center of the back under the yoke; at the shoulder seams; and where the sleeves and cuffs meet. Pleats always look dressier, on trousers as well as on shirts, and the additional fabric that a pleat provides allows for generally freer movement.

•**Mother-of-Pearl Buttons:** Not only pleasing to the eye, with a rich, pearly sheen, mother-of-pearl buttons are also more durable than plastic buttons.

•**Removable Collar Stays:** Collar stays are plastic strips that keep the collar points stiff. Better shirts have removable stays, because they can melt and bend when a shirt is cleaned.

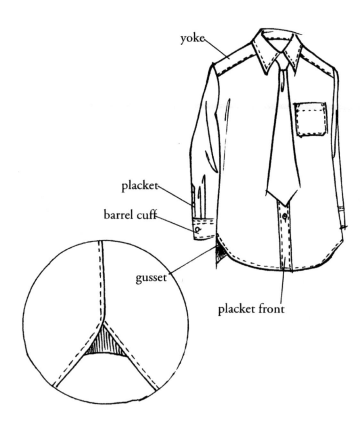

yoke

placket

barrel cuff

gusset

placket front

There are other details to check on a shirt, but experts disagree on their usefulness as indicators of quality.

Many say that a *gusset* (a small piece of fabric—usually triangular—attached where each of the two side seams meet) strengthens the seams. For Turnbull & Asser, Thomas Pink and other fine shirtmakers, the gusset is a signature style of their shirts. Others maintain it's an unnecessary and bulky detail.

A button on the *sleeve placket* (the opening of the sleeve fabric near the cuff), especially if matched with a horizontal buttonhole, is said by some to be another sign of a well-made shirt: the button keeps the placket closed, concealing the skin of a man's forearm. Others, however, hold that, these days, many mediocre shirts have placket buttons, because they are inexpensive to attach. Moreover, quite a few fine shirtmakers don't attach buttons at all because their shirt plackets are short and don't open.

Mr. Sahmanian says that a placket button is a must on a sleeve with a French cuff, which is merely pinched together by a cuff link but is optional on a sleeve with a barrel cuff, which folds the fabric over on itself. "If you wear a French cuff, you need a button on the sleeve placket, because a French cuff doesn't close as much as a barrel cuff," he says.

Split Yoke

Some shirtmakers maintain that a better shirt's *yoke* (the fabric across the back of the shoulders) is *split* down the center, though they differ on why. Some argue the two pieces of fabric are angled downward to complement the natural slope of the shoulders and provide a better fit than straight-across yokes. But Mr. Sahmanian says that the split yoke is meant only to provide a precise fit for the shoulders' width.

Custom-made shirts seem like an extravagance. Are they worth the expense and time?

The fit and the cotton of a well-made custom shirt are superior to those of a ready-made shirt. Of course, you'll pay for that quality—generally, each custom-made shirt will cost at least twice as much as the most expensive off-the-rack shirt. And the usual minimum order is six shirts. Also, it can take more than a month for your shirts to be made. Moreover, buying a custom-made shirt is not as simple as buying its packaged counterpart in the store. Getting fit for a custom shirt usually requires several visits to the tailor, because a custom-made shirt is a unique shirt. The fabric is cut especially to your measurements at the collar, chest, wrist, and so forth. You'll choose each stylistic detail: collar type, color, pattern, pocket, monogram, etc. Take, for example, cuff style: barrel with a double or single button? Or French cuff? Edges straight or rounded? Turnbull & Asser offers at least eight styles of cuff. And 800 fabrics from which to choose.

Many custom shirtmakers offer laundering services and will make repairs, such as for worn collars, and will replace buttons.

So, yes, a custom-made shirt does offer benefits. But is this costly indulgence for you? If you revel in fine fabrics and intriguing patterns, are fastidious about fit, and if you can afford a custom shirt's substantial price, then you may be just the sort to order bespoke shirts. Mr. deVaney says custom-shirt buyers are interested in fabrics and are frustrated because they don't find exactly what they want in ready-made shirts.

You also might be better served by a bespoke shirt if you have a pronounced physical attribute, or are very tall or short, and off-the-rack shirts are not commonly made in your measurements.

However, you may want to consider an option that falls between a ready-made and a bespoke shirt known as a *made-to-measure* shirt.

Made-to-measure shirts

BUYING A BESPOKE SHIRT:

First, you choose your fabric. You choose your collar; the kind of cuffs that you want to wear; whether you want a pocket or no pocket; whether you want a monogram or no monogram. Then we take your measurements—including chest, collar, yoke, sloping shoulders or square shoulders, height.
—*Gregory deVaney, CEO, Turnbull & Asser*

You try it on, we both criticize the hell out of it; we re-do the fabric; we make another one, which you have an option of not taking until you're absolutely, completely satisfied; and then the shirtmaker will make your shirts the same as the one you were satisfied with.
—*Alexander S. Kabbaz, custom shirtmaker*

are, in essence, ready-made shirts that are then altered to fit you more precisely at your waist, sleeve and collar. In this way, made-to-measure shirts are somewhat similar to made-to-measure suits. They have cardboard patterns already cut to standard sizes. The pattern is then adjusted to fit you. But the adjustments that can be made are limited, according to Mr. Kabbaz. (Note that sometimes made-to-measures are called custom-made, so beware.)

Made-to-measure shirts should fit better than ready-made shirts, and you have the same choice of fabrics that you have with custom-mades. They are cheaper than bespoke shirts, but more expensive than ready-made shirts. A minimum order of about a half-dozen shirts usually is required.

How should my shirt be worn with my tie and jacket?

James Mullen, co-founder of London's Thomas Pink, describes the space where the collar, lapels and tie converge as the "magic triangle" because of its visual importance: it is at the front and center of your outfit. Ideally, the rear of your shirt collar should rise 1/2 inch above your suit coat collar. The top of the collar's points should meet above the tie knot; there should be no empty space. The collar points should rest flat on the shirt front, either under or outside the coat's lapels. Try to coordinate the tie's width with the width of the jacket's lapels. No need to take out the measuring tape. Just glance in the mirror with proportionality in mind. Most ties are between 3 and 4 inches wide, which is a safe width to carry you through the changes of fashion.

Is a shirt with a French-front dressier than one with a standard front?

A *French-front* (a shirt with concealed buttons; also known as a *fly-front*) is not dressier than a *plain-front* or *placket-front* shirt (the two standard shirt fronts). It simply is a different style. "A French-front is more of a fashion shirt than a classic conservative shirt," says Sulka's Mr. Heaney.

French-Front

Placket-Front

What are the classic formalwear shirts?

See Formalwear chapter.

I've heard that a T-shirt should be worn underneath a dress shirt. Why?

Yes, a T-shirt should be worn under your dress shirt *especially* on hot days. A T-shirt prevents perspiration from darkening and staining your dress shirt and also helps prevent your chest from showing through thin shirt fabric or being revealed by an open collar.

How should I clean my shirts?

Shirtmakers recommend that shirts be washed by hand or by machine in luke-warm water. Don't dryclean your shirts—the chemicals are hard on the fabric and can turn shirts yellow. If you take your shirts to a drycleaner, make sure they are laundered, not drycleaned. And use little or no starch: starch ruins shirts by making the cotton fibers brittle and eventually causing them to break, which leads to frayed threads. "Starch will literally halve the life of your shirt," warns Mr. Kabbaz. And, of course, clean your shirts after each wearing.

To prevent deodorant stains, wait for the deodorant to dry before putting on your shirt. If your shirts do get stains from the combination of perspiration and deodorant, experts urge washing the shirt promptly rather than letting it languish until you wash the rest of the clothes. And try bleach.

Also, remember to remove collar stays before you clean your shirt, or they'll get lost or become attached to the fabric by the heat, if drycleaned.

When I iron my shirts, they are never as crisp as I'd like them to be. Is there a proper way to iron shirts?

It is seldom that you will match the professional's technique of pressing a shirt. But if you do iron your shirts yourself, use a hot iron on a damp shirt. Finer cotton weaves should be treated with lower heat than coarser weaves. Your collar will be seen even if you wear a suit or sport coat, so it is crucial to iron it properly. Iron the collar away from the points, the Thomas Pink shirtmakers advise, to avoid "unsightly creasing at the front of the collars." Iron pockets upward toward the openings. Pleats are best ironed flat, in the direction of the fold.

NECKWEAR

A tie is the most expressive item that a man has in his wardrobe.

—Gerald Andersen, executive director,
Neckwear Association of America

Style is not necessarily limited to clothes. It's how you carry yourself. Cary Grant, Gregory Peck, Jimmy Stewart—these men embodied style. It was more than skin-deep.

—Tom Kalenderian, executive vice president,
men's merchandizing, Barneys New York

The necktie is like the first violin in an orchestra: it occupies center stage, and when a mistake is made, it is noticed. So select your ties with care.

Keep in mind that the necktie is the only article of men's clothing meant solely for ornamentation. It allows you to express your personality through indulgence in sumptuous hues and designs in an otherwise staid business wardrobe. So, enjoy the varieties of colors, fabrics, textures and patterns. Wear the tie as it is meant to be worn: as a sort of personal signature.

It is unfortunate that many men don't see ties this way. They consider the necktie a symbol, like the gray flannel suit, of stultifying conformity. However, ties offer almost unlimited freedom for self-expression. In fact, there is a tie to match the subtlest nuance of one's mood. Feeling dapper and gentlemanly? Don an elegant, navy-blue woven silk tie graced with small white polka dots. Sporty? Knot up that one with the scrappy terriers racing across it. The trick is to make certain that your tie's "statement" not only reflects your taste, but is also appropriate for the office, the wedding, or whatever the occasion. Classic ties, with their unfailing elegance and many styles, admirably serve both the requirements of social customs and the individual's desire for self-expression.

This chapter will show you how to assemble a wardrobe of ties that possess enduring style, and how you can wear them to best advantage.

What's most important to know when buying a tie?

It may sound obvious, but the most important thing is that you like how a tie looks. Buy the tie that appeals to you, the tie that catches your eye. Which is how we all choose ties, anyway.

However, your tie should not only strike your fancy, but should also be appropriate for the occasions at which you'll be wearing it. You may take a shine to that hula-girls-and-palm-trees number at the store, but unless you work in a Hawaiian souvenir shop, don't buy it.

Your tie also should coordinate well with your suits and jackets; therefore, when you shop for a tie, don't evaluate it as it's displayed, with other ties on a table. Consider how the tie's colors, design, fabric and width would complement a specific suit or jacket. Try to wear the clothes you have in mind to pair it with. Memory can deceive. The most striking tie may not match anything in your closet. If you're not wearing a suit or jacket when you're buying a tie, compare the tie to those in the store that most resemble the ones you own and determine whether they work well together. But note that even subtle differences between the tailored clothing in your closet and those in the shop can lead to less-than-optimal neckwear purchases—you may discover that the gold stripes of the tie which looked so luxurious against the blazer in the store suddenly appear a bit pallid against your slightly lighter-hued sport jacket.

Many of my ties already look like antiques or are too garish for my current job. What are some tried-and-true classic ties I can stock up on?

Among the gaudy ties filling racks and covering the tables of the world's haberdasheries, there are several classics. These are ties that will remain elegant as long as men wear the *four-in-hand* (the modern necktie, so-named, according to legend, because it resembled the reins that British coach drivers used when driving four horses). Below are descriptions of the most well-known classic ties. You'll recognize most of these ties by their patterns, rather than by their fabrics, colors or weaves.

• **Solid:** A tie of one color. This is among the most versatile of ties. Solids wear well with both dressy suits and casual sport jackets, and with a wide range of solid-color and patterned suits. Some experts recommend burgundy or navy blue, because they are among the most versatile colors.

•**Dot:** As the name implies, a tie with repeating dots. Small dots, known as *pin dots*, are considered among the most subtle patterns. As with all patterns, however, the bigger the dot, the more casual the look: larger dots, known as *polka dots*, are not as elegant. After all, polka dots that are too big are more appropriate for clown suits than for pinstripe suits.

•**Foulard (or Ivy League):** A tie with evenly spaced, geometric images. A dot tie, for example, is a type of foulard. But foulards include patterns of squares, oblongs and any other shape. The foulard, according to Brooks Brothers, was brought back to the United States from England by the company's senior partner, Francis G. Lloyd, in 1890, and it quickly gained the popularity that it retains more than a century later.

•**Geometric:** A tie with abstract designs. A geometric tie differs from a foulard in that its shapes are not evenly spaced—they run throughout the tie and are often small and interconnected.

•**Striped:** Diagonally striped ties originated in 19th century Britain. *Rep(p)* ties, popularized after World War I by the Duke of Windsor, bore the colors and patterns of the wearer's army regiment, such as the Grenadier Guards. *Old School* ties—also striped— bore those of the wearer's public school. Today, however, striped ties have mostly lost such associations.

In Britain, the stripes run downward from left to right, while in the United States, the stripes run downward from right to left, a holdover, according Brooks Brothers, from when the company introduced the pattern to America in 1920. The company still offers the same Rep pattern John Brooks brought back from Britain those many years ago, called the "Brooks Brothers' No. 1" Rep (it has three alternating colors: a background color and a double

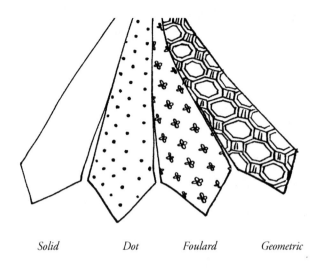

Solid   *Dot*   *Foulard*   *Geometric*

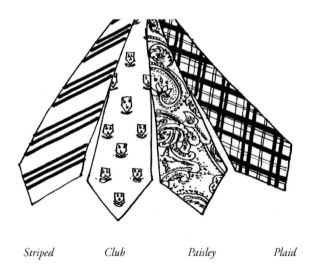

Striped   *Club*   *Paisley*   *Plaid*

stripe backed by a third color). "That is a total classic," enthuses Jarlath Mellett, executive vice president, design director, at Brooks Brothers. However, there's no need to stick with old No. 1—Rep ties encompass any tie that has stripes.

•**Club:** A tie with a repeating pattern of small images, usually of sport or nature, such as tennis racquets or game birds. Club ties originally served to identify members of Britain's private clubs because they bore club emblems. "Club ties add a bit of whimsy," says Paul Stuart. For this reason, be warned: not all club ties should be worn with business attire.

•**Paisley:** A tie with a curved teardrop, or *paisley*, pattern running throughout. Paisleys are tricky—if the pattern and colors are subdued, they can be dressy, but bolder paisleys are best left for more casual outfits. The paisley name derives from the Scottish mill town of Paisley, famous in the 19th century for its paisley-patterned shawls. In the 1930s, the paisley pattern was first used to decorate ties. The paisley design (which represented a date palm, a fertility symbol) originated in ancient Babylonia then spread to India and beyond.

•**Plaid:** A tie with a *plaid* pattern (lines or bars of at least two colors crossing at right angles). A casual tie, it is made of cotton or linen for summer and of wool for cooler weather. Plaid patterns originated in Scotland and were used on shawls and kilts. A *shepherd's plaid* has black and white checks. The most common plaid, *tartan*, originally was used to represent clans of Scotland's Highlands. Tartans have at least three bars of color crossing at right angles.

When I dress for the office, should I wear only those ties that fit into one of these eight categories?

Not necessarily. They may be classics, but they aren't required wearing, and they're not the only classics. *Knit* ties (loosely woven ties with square-ended aprons), for example, are extremely versatile, especially in solid black. Furthermore, non-traditional patterns are acceptable now, even on Wall Street and in traditional professions, such as law and accounting. That a man should wear only traditional ties is no longer true: "I don't think that's applicable any more, I don't think its current," says Mr. Heaney, of Sulka. However, if you do venture away from the classics, keep the ties tasteful. Resist "conversational" ties—those ties with hula girls and palm trees. They may elicit conversation, but of an unwelcome sort.

Are some of these classics considered dressier than others? And what makes a tie "casual"?

As noted above for the dot tie, a good rule of thumb is that the tie becomes dressier as the pattern becomes smaller. Again, it's a matter of common sense: big, bold shapes are louder than smaller ones. Formalwear, by contrast, is composed of solid white and black. Ties of most solid colors are impeccably stylish. Reps are generally sober enough to match well with most suits and most occasions and are considered the classic tie for business. Plaids and large paisley patterns are generally not considered dressy because they are so busy.

In addition to color and pattern, the *texture* of the fabric also determines whether a tie is casual or dressy: the rougher the weave, the more casual the tie. And printed ties are more casual than woven ties.

How do woven ties differ from printed ties?

The difference between a woven tie and a printed tie lies in how the tie's pattern is created, and all ties fall into one category or the other. The pattern of a woven tie is created by the weave of different colored threads. The pattern of a printed tie, on the other hand, is printed onto the fabric. Take a close look at a woven and a printed four-in-hand or bow tie and you'll observe the difference. And, by the way, patterns on some ties are printed onto a woven pattern, which, according to Mary Beth Walsh of Robert Talbott, is a more European look.

Wovens may have the same vivid colors as a print, but printed designs can be more complex than woven designs. Wovens are generally considered a bit dressier than prints. "There's no difference, necessarily, in quality," says Gerald Andersen, executive director of the Neckwear Association of America, an industry group in New York. "You generally pay more for a woven than you will for a print because wovens are more expensive to produce. But you cannot execute certain kinds of designs in a woven that you can with a print."

Is it improper to wear a tie that's not pure silk with a business suit?

All of your ties need not be made of pure silk, but most ties in your closet should be. For all-season businesswear and casualwear, you can't err when you wear a pure silk tie. The luxurious sheen of a silk tie will best accompany the dressy look of most of your suits. However, ties of silk blended with wool, linen, cotton or other natural fibers also can be appropriate for the office, as long as they have a relatively hard finish.

Ties of pure wool, cashmere, linen or cotton are, for the most part, seasonal and more casual because of their softer finish. So reserve those heavy, fuzzy wool ties for autumn walks in the park, or for other cool-weather, out-of-the-office activities. Wear them with your heavy wool sport jacket or suit, which will complement their greater heft. Cotton and linen ties? Pull them out for that lunch at that sidewalk bistro in the warmer months. They'll best be worn with similarly lightweight, summery fabrics.

How many ties should I own for a core wardrobe?

A dozen or so of the classic ties will get a man comfortably through a five-day week at the office. You want enough ties so that you are not forced to wear the same ties with each suit or sport coat each week. In other words, you want more than one tie for each outfit. Also, you want to allow your ties to rest between wearings.

Buy ties that bear just a few, versatile colors, such as blue, burgundy, yellow or red, and that have simple patterns. Ties of a solid color are especially adaptable. The object is to avoid your ties clashing with the patterns and colors of your shirts, sport jackets or suits. In general, it is best that a core tie wardrobe be composed of silk ties. However, a few ties of cotton or wool or of silk-blends will help take you stylishly through the seasons.

How can I recognize a well-made tie?

First, examine the quality of the fabric—that's primarily what you pay for. Cheap silks and synthetics always look shabby. Then, examine the quality of the craftsmanship. Mary Beth Walsh, of Robert Talbott, says: "First of all, it's the *hand* [the weight and texture of the fabric]. Then you want to flip it over and look at the guts of it."

•**Fabric:** The hand of the fabric should be substantial, although some of the finest silk ties (and silk blends) possess a coarse texture because of the thickness of the weave. And you want that thick weave—that's what gives your tie its luxurious appearance. It also gives it the strength to resist wrinkles. "You torture a tie when you knot it," says Paul Stuart, and ties must be sturdy enough withstand such cruelty unscathed. Moreover, a thicker tie produces a knot large enough to fill the gap between the points of a shirt's spread collar. A substantial hand also helps ensure that the knot won't slide down.

Note, though, that printed ties often have a silkier hand than wovens, because the patterns are printed onto the tie rather than woven into the tie. Therefore, a tie that slithers between your fingers may—but also may not—be a sign that it is made of fine fabric. Fine cotton and linen ties have a hand that is lighter than that of silk ties.

•**Lining:** This is the woolly, inside strip around which the *shell fabric* (the fabric of the outside of the tie, also known as the *envelope*) of the tie is sewn, and it contributes to the hand of the tie. If the silk is a thick weave, the lining should be lightweight, and vice-versa. "You can just tell when you feel a tie if the lining has some body to it. If it does, it's going to tie a good knot, it's going to keep its shape," says Sulka's Mr. Heaney. "If it doesn't have a fairly substantial lining, it's not going to hold up." Moreover, the lining should run all the way through the neckband of the tie. "Otherwise, you're going to get a really skinny, skimpy knot," warns Ms. Walsh.

Finally, a substantial lining produces a *roll* (a slight curve at the tie's edges) which adds a fuller look to the tie. Any stripes or bars in the lining, contrary to the myth that they indicate quality, actually indicate only the weight of the lining; the more stripes, the heavier the lining.

•**Print:** "Looking at a printed fabric is like looking at a photograph: if it's not crisp and sharp, it's probably a cheap print," advises Mr. Andersen. A poor print also may mean that the silk is of inferior quality.

•**Three-Piece Construction:** Well-made ties are composed of three pieces of silk: the *apron* (the wide front-piece); the *neckband* (the center-piece); and the *backpiece* (the tie's narrow end). Ties made of only two pieces, experts say, won't drape properly.

•**Bias Cut:** The fabric of a tie should be cut on a *bias* (a 45-degree angle). A bias cut is said to keep the fabric from twisting on itself when you wear the tie. The bias can be detected by draping the apron from your fingers: if the tie hangs still, with no twisting, it is cut on the bias. The finest ties are bias-cut on the shell, lining and tipping.

•**Bartack:** The bartack is a thread that is stitched across the main seam for reinforcement. A tie should have two bartacks, one on each end. Beware of bartacks made with merely a few back-and-forth stitches, which are likely to unravel. You want the threads tightly twisted, which strengthens the bind.

•**Slipstitch:** The slipstitch is a long thread that runs the length of the tie, like a spine, and keeps the tie's shape. It is secured to the shell-fabric by a knot at each end. You can usually find it by spreading open the aprons. "Without a slipstich," says Paul Stuart, "a tie is static from one end to the other; it's not going to move. It won't drape properly, and you'll have a hard time tying it. It's the single most important factor in the making of the tie, because it determines how the tie lays."

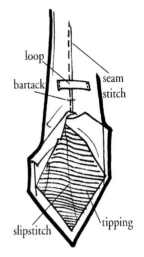

•**Loop:** Many excellent tie manufacturers use their label for a *loop* (the strip of fabric that you slide the backpiece through when you wear your tie). However, it's a nice touch if the loop is of *self-fabric* (the same fabric) as the rest of the tie. "It's another sign of a well-made tie," says Paul Stuart. Moreover, the loop should be sewn on by hand, rather than by machine, for a stronger hold. You can tell that a loop has been attached by hand when it is stitched to the shell-silk by its four corners, rather than by vertical stitches across its edges. Some loops are not only of self-fabric, but also have edges that are sewn into the main seam—another sign of sturdy craftsmanship.

•**Label:** Many manufacturers put their labels into service as loops, as noted above, but others sew their labels discreetly on the backpiece. A minority of better tiemakers go to the expense of printing their labels on the silk of the backpiece, rather than sewing on a label.

•**Tipping:** Tipping is the bit of fabric visible in the opening at the back of the aprons, and, like the lining, it should run the length of the tie. Tipping was once of silk but most tipping now is made of artificial fabrics. The tipping on a minority of better ties is of the same fabric and pattern as the shell, making the front and back of the apron almost indistinguishable. "I would look for a tipping that is a little more ornate," says Ms. Walsh. She adds that when

• **Fabric:** The hand, or feel, of the tie fabric should be both substantial and luxurious.

• **Lining:** The weight of the lining should complement weight of shell fabric, and be sturdy enough to produce a roll.

• **Print:** A pattern that is printed on the tie fabric should be both crisp and sharp.

• **Three-Piece Construction:** Ties of superior quality are made from three pieces: the apron, the neckband and the backpiece.

• **Bias Cut:** Fabric should be cut on a 45-degree angle.

• **Bartack:** A tie should have two tightly twisted bartacks.

• **Slipstitch:** There should be a slipstitch running the length of the tie, in order to maintain a proper drape.

• **Loop:** Look for a loop that is made of self-fabric and that is sewn on by hand.

• **Label:** The label may serve as a loop; labels on a few of the best ties are printed on the backpiece.

• **Tipping:** Tipping should run length of tie; better tipping is made from self-fabric.

• **Seam Stitch:** Hand-stitching along the seam stitch is a sign of a well-made tie.

the maker's name is printed into the tipping, it means the maker owns that silk pattern, so that it is unique.

• **Seam Stitch:** The seam stitch is the thread that holds together the main seam. Stitching on hand-made ties is not quite uniformly spaced, although such uneven stitching can be duplicated by machine.

What's the best classic tie money can buy?

A *seven-fold* tie is the most costly, but they're not available at many shops. Seven-folds are pricey because they are hand-made from one large piece (about a square yard) of pure silk, unsupported by a wool lining, with the silk folded seven times over itself. Seven-folds are made the way ties were made before the advent of modern construction methods in the 1920s. Most people probably won't recognize a seven-fold for the rarity it is. "There's no benefit to wearing one, it's a luxury item," says Mr. Andersen, of the Neckwear Association of America. A seven-fold tie costs about twice as much as an expensive conventional tie, according to Robert Talbott, one of the few tie makers that produce seven-folds.

What are the different tie knots?

Whatever the shape of your collar, your tie knot should fit snugly between the collar's points: If it lifts the points or strains the buttons, your knot is too large; if it leaves a lot of exposed fabric between the points, it's too small. For most collars, use the knot you've been tying most of your life: the *four-in-hand* knot, which shares the name of the tie on which the knot is used. It's been the most common knot for decades—probably because it's simple to tie, and its narrow, triangular shape fits well in smaller collars, such as tab and pin collars. Loosely wrapped, it can adapt to all but the widest spread collars. There are other knots, notably the Windsor and half-Windsor.

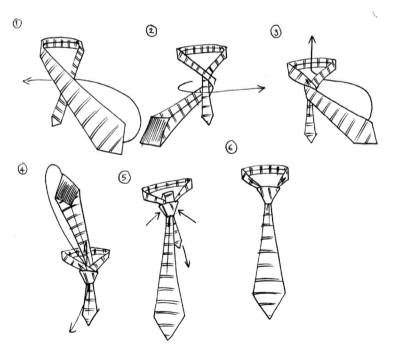

How to tie a Four-in Hand Knot

•**Windsor Knot:** The Windsor knot (named after the Duke of Windsor, who is said to have made it fashionable) provides balance to broad lapels and padded shoulders. "The Windsor, which creates a larger, triangular shaped knot, works very well with spread collars but does not look good with ties that are very heavy," because the knot will be too large, says Mr. Andersen.

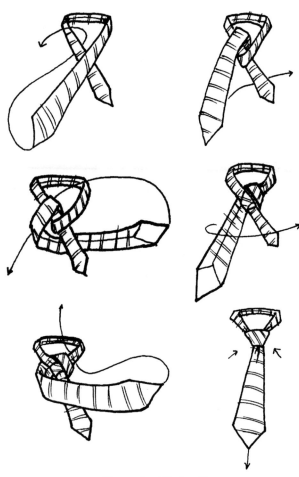

How to tie a Windsor Knot

Small men may be overwhelmed by the Windsor, while large men may find it balances their physique.

•**Half-Windsor Knot:** The half-Windsor is, as its name suggests, a bit smaller than the Windsor. It is also a bit larger than the four-in-hand. Best worn with spread collars.

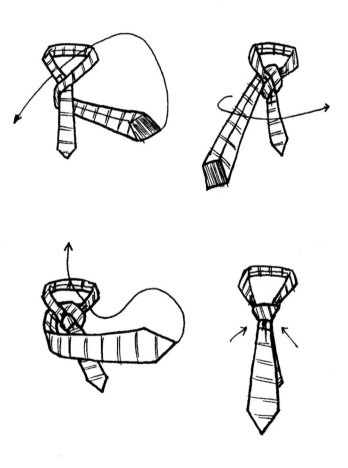

How to tie a Half-Windsor Knot

Is there a proper way to wear a tie?

•**Length:** Regardless of how you knot it, your tie should hang to the center of your belt buckle or, if you are wearing suspenders, to the waistband of your trousers. A shorter tie will expose a patch of your shirt front, which will lure eyes to your midriff. For heavy men this is especially undesirable. If your tie drapes below your belt, your appearance will be unbalanced.

Ties are not made in standard sizes. They range from about 53 to 57 inches. If your ties tend to be too long, try wearing them inside your trousers, or try wearing looser knots. Or tie a Windsor or half-Windsor knot. If your ties are too short, wear a sweater to conceal it. Many men wear their trousers on their hips rather than on their waist, and if your tie tends to be short, make sure your trousers are resting high enough. The backpiece of the tie should be long enough to slip through the loop after you knot the tie.

•**Dimple:** After you've formed your knot but before you've pushed it into place, you create the *dimple* (the small indentation of fabric just below the center of the knot). The dimple lends a tie an elegance of line, an illusion of depth. It's also a detail that will be noticed because it's so near your face. An easy way to make a dimple: press in the fabric just below the knot with your finger as you knot up the tie, forcing the fabric to pinch into proper shape.

•**Arch:** Finally, your tie should have a slight, forward arch, or thrust, below the knot. Like the dimple, the arch of a tie adds a touch of elegance to your appearance. When men wore three-piece suits, the vest supported the tie, forcing it a bit forward. Since the three-piece suit has become an endangered species, the arch has become—again, like the dimple—an often-unrealized ideal. Nevertheless, you can achieve that arch by wearing a tie clip or a tie pin; a shirt with a tab or pin collar; or, of course, a vest.

Can I have a tie altered?

Yes, ties can be narrowed, widened and shortened. But if you do choose to alter a tie, go to good a seamstress or tailor, because the tie has to be taken apart and put together again. The best way to avoid having a tie altered is simply to buy the right tie in the first place: that is, a tie between about 3 or 4 inches in width. This has proven to be a fairly standard width. Avoid very narrow and very wide ties, and you'll avoid alterations.

BOW TIES

Butterfly Bow Tie

Is it appropriate to wear a bow tie to the office?

Be cautious about about wearing that bow tie to the office, no matter how natty it looks on you. This holds true even though the bow tie is a classic style of men's neckwear, as perfectly acceptable for business as a four-in-hand. Bow ties, however, are rarely worn, so wear one only if you are not afraid to attract attention. "Bow ties should be worn by a more confident person," cautions Karen Albano, a sales associate at Robert Talbott. Winston Churchill, for example, wore a trademark blue-and-white dot bow tie. So, it's not that you would be committing a sartorial *faux pas* if you wore that bow tie to your office; it's a matter of prudence.

Is there any way a bow tie could benefit my wardrobe?

Well, yes: they won't bulge under your sweater. And they won't stray into your soup or to other places where a tie has no business—such as around a doctor's examining table. In fact, for men in medicine and other professions that require a bit of dressiness but also demand physical activity, a bow tie is worth considering as an alternative to the four-in-hand. Moreover, the very fact that a bow tie may brand one as somewhat of an eccentric is, to some, its attraction. It is traditional, yet still a bit different. "Bow ties have a little more individuality," says Mr. Andersen. "It's not the uniform, and that's a large part of the appeal."

What are my options in classic bow ties?

Bow ties come in as many patterns and fabrics as the four-in-hand. But there are only three classic shapes for bow ties. All are proper for daywear or for formalwear.

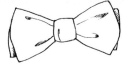

•**Butterfly:** The butterfly has ends that flair as they extend outward to straight edges. The most common shape of bow tie, the butterfly appeared in the early years of this century as a wider version of the traditional bow tie. In the days when more rigid rules of dress dictated a man's attire, the bow tie and four-in-hand were considered proper formal daywear.

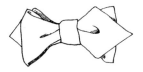

•**Bat's Wing:** The bat's wing is narrower than the butterfly. Its edges are pointed.

•**Straight (or Thistle):** A tie that, as its name suggests, extends straight outward. The narrowest bow tie and the least common style of the three. Edges are usually straight, but they can be pointed.

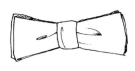

How is a bow tie knotted?

It's been said that a bow is tied the same way that you tie your shoes, except you have to imagine your shoe on your neck. The confusing part is looking in the mirror. Simply focus on what you're doing, don't glance in the mirror, and just tie the bow. Most bow ties have adjustable sizebands; before you buy one *without* a sizeband, make sure it fits by trying it on. Typically, sizebands have necksizes printed on them or woven in them (although the numbers aren't so important). Once you adjust the sizeband appropriately, you create the knot.

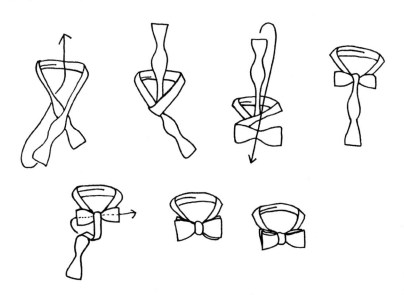

How to Tie a Bow Tie

Knotting a bow tie seems complex—I'd rather wear a clip-on bow tie instead. Will anyone notice?

If you can tie your shoes and if you can knot a four-in-hand, then you can knot a bow tie. Besides, clip-on ties are gauche, and you won't be fooling anyone. "I can spot them a mile away, because they have a rigid, packaged look," says Mr. Andersen.

Is there a correct size for a bow tie?

Keep your bow tie about as wide as your shirt collar, neither too small nor too large. Any smaller, and you'll look too large for it; any broader, and it will look clownish.

Too Narrow   *Too Wide*   *Just Right*

Can I wear bow ties with both single- and double-breasted suits? And what about with button-down collars?

Bow ties are wonderfully adaptable. They are appropriate with single- and double-breasted suits (Harry Truman wore his with a double-breasted). They also go well with sport coats, three-piece suits and shirts with button-down collars.

Which ties are proper for black-tie and white-tie affairs?

See Formalwear chapter.

ASCOTS

What, exactly, is an ascot?

You probably already know what an ascot looks like: it's that flamboyant silk neck scarf that old-time Hollywood directors wore while shouting commands through megaphones. Film stars appeared in ascots with smoking jackets. The ascot exudes a more casual elegance than the modern four-in-hand, although many years ago the ascot was considered formal day wear, and it is still worn at formal daytime weddings. The ascot gets its name from England's Ascot-Heath horse races, held annually since the 1770s, where men wore this neck cloth.

Ascot patterns are the same as those of four-in-hands, because an ascot is a form of necktie. However, the ascot, unlike the four-in-hand, has two wide aprons, and no lining. The aprons are connected by a narrow, pleated centerpiece that wraps around the neck. Traditionally, ascots were worn with a *wing collar* (a collar with points that jut outward, and which is used for formalwear) and the aprons draped outside the shirt. They were fastened through the knot (which was sometimes concealed by the top apron) by a pearl or gold stickpin. Today, ascot aprons usually are tucked into the collar, with one apron folded over the knot and let to lie without a stickpin. Most ascots are made of silk, but they can be found in other fabrics, such as cotton. Ascots of wool and cashmere, with their heavier hand, work best with heavier wool jackets.

I like the sporty stylishness of an ascot, but will it appear a bit of an affectation?

Ascots can add either insouciance or foppishness to your attire, depending upon whom you ask. Like bow ties, ascots are rare and so invite attention. "You should wear an ascot only if you feel comfortable in an ascot," says New York clothier Jay Kos. "If you're trying too hard, it's going to look ridiculous. And that goes for any article of clothing."

How and when are ascots worn?

Wear your ascot directly against your neck. Tuck the blades inside your open collar—and you may wear it with any collar style. Wear it with casual yet refined attire. An ascot is best worn at that country club lunch or at that Sunday at that steeplechase.

How to Tie an Ascot

CARE

How should I store my ties?
Hang all your ties, except for knits, which should be either folded or rolled to prevent stretching.

What's the best way to remove creases in a tie?
The best way is to hold an iron about an inch over the crease and let the steam pass over it while you smooth out the crease with your hands. However, never iron a tie flat, because it will squash the roll along the edges. "You'll have it look flat as a pancake, and it will shine and ruin the look of the silk," says Andrew Tarshis, president of Tiecrafters, a Manhattan tie-cleaning specialist since 1952, whose clients have included President Richard M. Nixon and United Nations Secretary General Perez deCuellar, among many others. Mr. Tarshis also suggests hanging a tie near a shower.

"Gravity pulls out the wrinkles to some extent," he says.

Mr. Andersen, of the Neckwear Association of America, urges giving your tie a few days "rest" between wearings, to help the wrinkles smooth out. Experts also recommend that tie knots should not be too tight.

Is there a proper way to remove my tie?

Always unknot your tie before removing it. Take off your tie by unknotting it in reverse, in order to minimize wear-and-tear.

Is there an effective way to remove spots and stains?

Ties have a way of getting into salads, pen ink and coffee. When your tie gets stained, first dab away any excess immediately after the spill using a damp, soft cloth, Mr. Tarshis recommends. "That's the only home remedy. The club soda myth is exactly that—a myth," he says, referring to the belief that applying club soda to a stain will remove it. Be careful not to put too much water on some silks, which may enlarge the spot.

If you can't remove the spot, don't send the tie to an ordinary drycleaner. Most drycleaners lack proper equipment to clean ties. Silk can lose its color and lustrous finish, and the roll can be flattened if improperly cleaned. Find a drycleaner that specializes in cleaning ties. A tie usually must be chemically hand-spotted first, and then drycleaned. Mr. Tarshis recommends a once-a-year general tie cleaning even if no specific staining occurs.

SHOES

Shoes are the foundation on which a man builds his out-fit. Most of us know they are one of the first things that catches the eye of a woman.

—Bruno Francois, president, J.M. Weston NY Inc.

Shoes, like the rest of your wardrobe, say a lot about your sense of style. A well-polished pair of cordovan oxfords, for example, signals your attention to detail and appreciation of quality. A battered pair of cheap shoes can tell the world less flattering things.

However, shoes must serve function as well as style. Poorly fitting shoes make life a misery. Even ancient man grasped the tension between footwear's form and function. Some shoes estimated to be as much as 8,000 years old that were found in Calloway County, Missouri, were comfortable-looking slip-ons made of grass, fiber and leather, yet also had modern design elements, such as heels, a sleekly shaped toe and straps to allow for a secure fit and easy removal. Even in that age, a man probably would have been be pleased to have shoes admired by the less well-shod.

Until the late 19th century, most shoes extended above the ankle to protect the wearer's feet from the elements and from mud in unpaved streets, and those cut below the ankle were worn with spats (ankle coverings attached to the shoe's instep). But by the early 20th century, when urban living became tidier, nearly all dress shoes were cut low and spats were done away with. Through this century, men's shoe designs have changed little. This chapter introduces the classic styles and explains how to wear them well with your clothes and how to recognize quality.

What are the classic shoe styles?

Most shoes fall into two groups: the *oxford*, and the *slip-on*.

Broadly speaking, the *oxford* (named after the British university, where it is said to have originated) embraces all lace-ups that are cut to the ankle and that have at least three lacing eyelets.

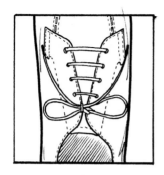

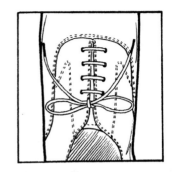

Blucher Lacing

Balmoral Lacing

Oxfords divide into two broad categories, differentiated by the styling of the lace-up area: the *blucher* (open throat lacing), and the sleeker, and therefore dressier, *balmoral* (closed throat, or "V" shaped lacing, named after the British royal family's castle in Scotland). Purists maintain that only the black cap-toe with a balmoral lace-up is a true oxford.

As a rule, lace-up shoes are the summit of dressiness short of formal pumps, and are acceptable businesswear around the world. But lace-ups also can be styled more casually, by use of rougher grain leather, a blucher rather than a balmoral, and other details.

The term *slip-on* covers a gamut of styles but is basically any shoe with no laces and a short *vamp* (the top part of the shoe extending to the toe). The *penny loafer*, described below, is the most popular slip-on, but many other styles exist, from the leather moccasin boat-shoe to fancy ones of crocodile skin, to the now-classic, and always chic, Gucci loafer, with its fine leather and a metal buckle across the upper. Slip-ons, which first became widely worn by college students in the United States in the 1930s, when they are said to have arrived from Norway, are very popular among Europeans, who have created a great many designs over the years, including the woven leather loafer. In Europe, slip-ons are often worn with suits, a combination that is still frowned on by many in the United States, given the slightly more casual nature of the slip-on compared with the oxford. But slip-ons are increasingly worn with suits in the United States. "Slip-ons are so comfortable, yet they're also very dressy," says Margaret Cordone, manager of Belgian Shoes. "It's a matter of personal taste as to whether you can wear a slip-on with a suit," she adds.

Whether you choose an oxford or a slip-on, stay with the classic styles; you'll find that they provide greater versatility than their trendy counterparts, advises Bruno Francois, President of J.M. Weston New York. "A pure classic shoe will definitely put the one who wears it on firm footing," he says. "It can be worn anywhere and is the best start and completion of any outfit; as an analogy, don't women wear a fine, classic piece of jewelry they like just about anywhere?"

The following describes the classic shoe styles you will probably encounter in shoe stores. Note, however, that many hybrids have developed. "You might see shoes that share styles and think, 'where does that belong?' As long as it is well-balanced, then it'll be all right," says Mr. Francois.

OXFORDS

•Plain Cap-Toe
Cap-toe shoes are distinguished by a separate piece of plain leather attached straight across the shoe's toe. They should be worn with dressy attire, and one would be hard-pressed to find a (male) investment banker or a lawyer who does not have a pair in his wardrobe. There are cap-toe bluchers and cap-toe balmorals. The slick, plain cap-toe balmoral is dressier than the blucher: it can even be appropriately worn with a tuxedo. "The plain cap balmoral is for safe, conservative men who enjoy its sleek lines and elegant grace," says Jeff McMillan, store manager at J.M. Weston New York.

•Brogue

A brogue is any dress shoe that includes *brogueing* (the tiny holes punched to form patterns). Brogueing can be done to varying degrees, from a *medallion* (brogueing on the toe) to *half brogues* and *full-brogues* (brogueing halfway, or entirely around the shoe). In general, the more perforations, the less dressy the shoe.

Wing-Tip:

The wing-tip is the most well-known brogue shoe. It gets its name from the brogue design on the toe, which resembles outstretched wings. The wing-tip has for many decades been the traditional style for businessmen, and for that reason this shoe carries too many "business" connotations for wearing casually or with formalwear.

•Plain-Toe Blucher

Blucher shoes, as noted above, are distinguished by an open-throat lace-up fastening, called a blucher. They are allegedly named after a

British lord who needed a specially designed lace-up to fit his less-than-perfect feet. The plain-toe blucher is a conservative but highly versatile shoe because of its simple elegance. It is popular among academicians and businessmen who favor a fuller shaped shoe in the lace-up area. Bluchers are also made with pebble-grain leather for a more casual look.

•Buck Oxford and White Buck-Oxford

Buck oxfords are classic summer shoes and are, in fact, plain-toe bluchers. Once commonly made of suede buckskin, they are now mostly made of tan suede calfskin. White buck oxfords are made from white-colored calfskin, but are not suede.

Both styles have a distinctive red, rubber sole, which lends a jaunty touch. Bucks are best worn with summer suits, such as those of poplin or seersucker, and are perfect for summer-weekend getaways, because they can accommodate almost any occasion, and are especially useful if you're not sure how casually one is expected to be dressed.

•Saddle
The saddle is an oxford blucher or balmoral characterized by a separate "saddle" shaped piece of leather at the instep. The saddle piece is often the same color and type of leather as that used for the rest of the shoe, or it can differ. Most golf shoes and many two-tone shoes (see below), for example, are saddle-style.

•Two-Tone
Two-tone shoes (or *spectator* shoes) are shoes made of leathers of at least two colors or two contrasting tones of the same color. They are typically white, with leather of black or brown. Spectator shoes

"add gaiety, smartness and elegance" to a wardrobe, says John Lobb, third-generation owner of London custom shoemaker John Lobb Ltd. But two-tone shoes are a week-end, or casual, shoe.

Two-tones come in the standard styles described above with pieces of leather of a different shade added. The wing-tip and the saddle shoe are among the most common styles which come in two tones. There are also three-toned shoes.

•Split-Toe: Introduced by J.M. Weston in the 1950s, the split-toe shoe is named for the vertical seam at the toe connecting two pieces of leather on the sides of the upper. These shoes have a third, separate piece of leather forming the top of the vamp. The split-toe detail is more of a feature than a shoe style; you will see the split-toe used on a variety of classic shoe styles, but it is most commonly on plain bluchers and loafers.

SLIP-ONS

•Penny Loafer

The penny loafer is a classic American shoe, and was particularly popular on Eastern university campuses in the 1930s, where students slipped coins into the slit on the band crossing the upper. Originally, men wore this as a weekend shoe (hence the name loafer) but the penny loafer is increasingly being worn with business suits.

•Tassel Loafer

The tassel loafer gets its name for its dangling leather florets, which make it dressier than the penny loafer. Once strictly a casual shoe, the tassel loafer has infiltrated acceptable business attire even more than the penny loafer, although many still think it is too casual for the office.

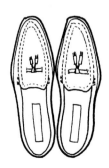

•Monk Strap

The monk strap (actually not a slip-on in the strictest sense) is named for the buckled leather strap across the upper. It is characterized by sleek lines and is almost always made in black calfskin with a buckle of silver or gold. The monk strap has been an enduring shoe style since the early part of this century, and some say it has an aristocratic air, although it also was widely worn by the hippie generation. A versatile shoe, the monk strap looks as sharp with casual clothes as it does

with suits. But be careful about wearing this shoe in staid offices: "Very few men can pull this look off," warns Mr. McMillan, of J.M. Weston. In more creative fields, however, the monk strap is likely to be admired. There are also double-strap models and monk strap boots.

•Formal Pump

The pump has been a fixture in formal wardrobes for more than a century, and it is still common at black-tie affairs. Formal footwear is always black and usually of *patent* leather (leather treated with a black, shiny varnish). However, patent leather and dainty elements, such as silk bows, are no longer required for black tie. Shoes of plain black calfskin are an acceptable substitute for patent leather.

I've noticed that a lot of shoes seem to be made in Britain and Italy. Are there differences among British, Italian and American shoes?

Italian-made shoes, in general, are known for narrow, sleek designs and thin soles. In contrast, British and American shoes are, for the most part, heavier-soled and double-soled. They usually have exposed, heavy *welts* (the layer of leather connecting the sole to the rest of the shoe), prominent stitching, longer vamps and bigger heels than their Italian counterparts. The sturdier design of British and American shoes resulted from the need for protection from cold, wet weather, and their heft complements generously cut British and American suits. Shoes made in Italy reflect that country's more temperate climate and are appropriate for lightweight clothes. There is no difference in quality among these styles; all three countries have fine shoe-making traditions. The superior choice largely depends on what shoe works best with the rest of your wardrobe, and the climate in which you wear it.

How many pairs of shoes—and which styles—belong in a core wardrobe?

The shoes that a man should own primarily depends on his profession and on his leisure lifestyle. A chef, for example, may need two pairs of comfortable boots and a pair of sneakers. An executive might need five dressy pairs of oxfords. A man who spends his weekends around the house with his family will probably want a different shoe than a man who spends his weekends at a country club. For most office workers, however, experts say three shoes is the minimum number to own.

John Isaacs, co-owner of Barrie Ltd., of New Haven, suggests: "Going from formal on down, the first is the black cap-toe with balmoral lacing in a regular-weight leather and a 1/4 inch-thick leather sole. This style can be worn with any traditional suit and even a tuxedo. Second, go with a pair of what I call the 'country club' type of shoe—the traditional, old-money shoe used with a suit or sport coat. This includes the tassel loafer, monk strap or penny loafer in black, brown or cordovan. The third category would be a more casual, everyday brown blucher oxford with a rubber sole. These casuals are best worn with khakis and a blazer, even jeans or corduroys and, in a pinch, you can use them with a suit. A casual of *NuBuck* [leather treated to create a nap similar to but not as soft as suede] or suede looks great with flannel slacks."

Are custom-made shoes worth the time and expense?

The vast majority of men have no need for custom-made shoes. You may want a pair, however, if you require a special fit or if you are among that minority of men who truly appreciate exquisitely crafted footwear—and can afford their stiff expense (into the thousands of dollars for a single pair). A pair of hand-made shoes also endures for decades, survives many resolings and, if the style is a classic, will remain elegant.

Mr. Lobb says that custom-made shoes benefit both the health of your feet and your sartorial style: "When [a shoe] is entirely handmade and fits properly, it will put a smile on your face," he says.

What makes some shoes dressier than others?

For all styles, black is dressier than cordovan and brown, which are dressier than tan and white. "Brown is considered more of a weekend shoe, or country shoe, than a black shoe, which is normally the color of a business shoe, although that's certainly changing in Europe," says Robert Willis, sales manager of Edward Green, a London custom shoemaker. Any other colors, such as blue, should be worn with caution and only with casual clothing. The simpler the shoe, the dressier; the more detail and embellishments (e.g., perforations, medallions, tassels, exposed stitching, etc.), the more casual the shoe. "The plain cap-toe is considered more formal than the wingtip," says Mr. Willis. Also, as mentioned earlier, lace-ups are more dressy than slip-ons, and balmoral lace-ups are more dressy than bluchers.

There is also a hierarchy of leathers. The finest calfskin, kidskin and cordovan usually are reserved for dressy shoes, the sort worn with business suits and formalwear. Suede and full-grain cowhide are usually used for more casual shoes. Other, more exotic skins, such as those of crocodile and alligator, are expensive, but are generally not appropriate for traditional business.

The following are descriptions of the most common types of shoe leathers:

THE HEART AND SOUL
OF A CUSTOM-MADE SHOE

First, I watch how someone walks, and try to find any peculiarities, like bow legs, which places the force on the outside of the foot. And, of course, I look for any unusual shapes of the foot. Then I take measurements, make a pattern, and then the last [a wooden model of the foot on which the shoe leather is shaped] is prepared. The last is made by hand and really is a piece of art unto itself.

Next, I cut the leather and make the uppers. The pieces are then stretched over the last and secured with tacks—this is called the pullover process. The stretched leather is then allowed to dry for about two or three weeks. The pullover process ensures that the leather contours to the shape of the last and that the leather will not bubble or lose shape later, when it is worn. It also makes the shoe hold better around the contours of the foot, for a more comfortable and secure fit.

The typical shoe has several components: the upper pieces of leather; an extra piece of leather in the heel, known as a heel stiffener; the lining; the leather insole; the welt [a strip of leather between the upper and the sole]; and the sole. We also insert a thick leather—not wood or metal—shank [a reinforcing strip] in the middle of the sole. The stitching of the bottom of the sole is invisible: an incision around the edge of the sole is made, the stitching is completed, then the flap from the incision is affixed over the stitching. Even at the top of the welt, the stitching is cleverly disguised by tamping the leather in tiny, radiating ruts between stitches.

Once the shoe is constructed, we heat hard wax over a flame and rub it into the shoe for a finish. A custom-made shoe can last up to twenty years, if well cared for. What you're really paying for is a pair of shoes which make you feel like you're walking in your bare feet.

—Roman Vaingauz, shoemaker, Vincent & Edgar

•**Alligator and Crocodile:** These skins—and other exotic skins such as those of lizards and snakes—are usually very costly. They are often used for slip-ons.

•**Calfskin:** Calfskin is among the most versatile and common of skins used for shoes, because it is soft and durable and breathes well. It can be given a shiny, matte or textured finish.

• **Cordovan:** A heavy, sinewy leather from horse's rump. Shoes of cordovan often are the most expensive and, when well taken care of, can last a lifetime. It has a characteristic mahogany color and glossy shine. The most durable leather available.

• **Full-Grain Leather:** Technically, any leather which has not been *split* (peeled into two layers). However, when you see "full-grain leather" on a label or stamped on the sole, the leather is probably from a cow. Cowhide is considered poor-quality material for uppers because of its toughness. It is usually split, and the result is used for lining or cheaper shoes. Cowhide is often altered by the use of coloring or by pressing textures into it (e.g., faux alligator).

• **Kidskin:** Leather from a young goat, known for its exquisite pliability and breatheability. Kidskin was more popular decades ago, and it is now uncommon in American-made men's shoes, but it is commonly used for custom shoes.

• **Suede:** Usually inside-out calfskin, which is treated in order to create a soft, chamois-like nap.

Are there any guidelines so that I'll always choose the best shoes to wear with my suits?

There are four general rules:

• First, keep your shoes darker than your suit. Light-toned shoes— and socks, for that matter—tend to draw attention to the foot. The shoe should accent the entire ensemble, not dominate it.

• Second, keep your shoes in the same color-family as your suit. So you'd wear black shoes with a navy blue suit or a gray suit, for example, and brown shoes with a brown suit. Some men, however, wear brown shoes with navy or charcoal suits. This is tricky territory. If you venture there, choose a pair of dark brown or cordovan shoes and make sure they are very well polished.

• Third, keep your shoes of roughly the same level of dressiness as your suits—so stay clear of moccasins, be wary of loafers unless your suit has a relaxed cut, and play it safe with oxfords.

• Fourth, keep your shoe style balanced with your suit's silhouette: no tiny Italian slip-ons with your Sack suit.

Is wearing boots with a suit bad form?

These days, most men would say yes. However, until almost a century ago, most business shoes were cut above the ankle. The lower-cut oxford became standard business attire only after modern life grew sufficiently tidy. Today, it goes without saying that snowboots are never appropriate indoors when wearing a suit, nor are cowboy boots or most other pointed boots. If you do choose to wear boots with your suit, make sure that the boot style, when partially covered by trouser, exhibits the smooth lines of a dressy oxford. You'll find, especially in the dead of winter, that black, highly polished monk straps or sleek, conventionally shaped boots, with soles of leather (not deep-treaded, rubber lug), will probably not draw disapproving comments or glances.

I walk to work and find leather-soled shoes uncomfortable. Are shoes with rubber soles too casual for business attire?

Yes, they are too casual. Traditionally, rubber soles were used for casual or sports shoes, and not for business shoes, and they remain incongruous with a suit. True, more and more men are wearing oxfords and slip-ons with rubber soles, even though these soles are less elegant than leather soles. And rubber soles do have merit: they are quiet and, therefore, good for the self-effacing man; they are not slippery on wet surfaces; and they tend to outwear leather soles. Most important, they cushion shock better than leather. Shoemakers are responding to the increasing acceptance of rubber by combining leather and rubber in the same sole for the best of both types. But leather-soled shoes are generally the proper shoe to wear with a suit.

Spotting Quality

How can I recognize a well-made pair of shoes?

•**Leather:** The quality of the shoe's leather is more important than the craftsmanship put into the shoe. Great leather has a smooth, consistent grain, is luxurious to the touch, and allows even the heaviest shoe to be pliable and resilient. Leathers are graded 1 through 5, with 1 signifying the highest quality, but these grades are not usually marked on shoes.

Remember, it is the quality of the leather, not the type of leather, that dictates the overall quality of a shoe. "First, check the leather closely, because what looks good in the shop window may appear less so close-up," advises Mr. Willis, of Edward Green.

•**Lining:** The lining of superior shoes is made of a high-quality calfskin and is cut so that the leather folds smoothly into the seams and edges.

•**Stitching:** The stitching should hold the shoe together but rarely be noticed, unless it is meant to be seen for design purposes. Stitching in dressy shoes should be inconspicuous; indeed, custom shoemakers almost completely conceal stitching on the top and bottom of the sole. Exposed knots on the inside of the shoe indicate poor craftsmanship and can cause discomfort. Even the stitching of the sole to welt should be recessed in the leather, and there should no loose threads. The more hand-stitching, the better. Hand-stitching is evident by stitches that are not identical. It allows seams to give a little more, making for a longer-lasting shoe. The threads are also less likely to unravel.

•**Soles:** The soles should be made of leather—they sound authoritative and tend to make men stand and walk with better posture. They are also more refined than their rubbery cousins. Leather

PERFECT IMPERFECTIONS

Beware of bottoms of soles which have been blackened—this usually means sloppy workmanship is being concealed. I like to see the workmanship in the sole of the shoe.

Avoid shoes with an overly glassy shine; frequently, this means the leather has been "corrected" or given a "brush off," which could mean imperfections or flaws in the leather are being covered up; a good hand-made shoe is not always perfect. A shoe should look clean, but the stitching may be a little imperfect. It's sort of strange, but that's true. Hand stitching lasts longer.

Look at where the lining meets the outer leather [the binding]. Here you can see if the workmanship is fine. It should look as clean as possible.

Lastly, place the shoe on a table top. The waist [the part of the sole under the instep] should be slightly rolled, or curved. The front of the heel should touch the table, the back should not. The tip of the toe should be just slightly up-turned. These basics in shoe balance are important to how a shoe will "walk."

—*John Isaacs, co-owner, Barrie Ltd.*

sole thickness varies with styles, and choosing one style over the other depends on your personal preference, the degree of formality of the rest of your outfit and the climate in which the shoes must survive. The soles of Italian slip-ons, for example, which are about 1/8 inch thick, are thinner than those of wing-tips and bluchers, which are up to 1/2 inch thick. Soles can be single, double or even triple-layered.

Most good soles are a pale-tan hue; this shows that the sole has not been colored to conceal imperfections. It also reveals the craftsmanship of exposed stitching. Soles also should be shaped as closely as possible to the foot, for a more comfortable and elegant shoe. They should be stitched, not glued to the shoe.

The best heels are made of leather. Many are reinforced with rubber and/or metal tips. Oversized heels can make a shoe uncomfortable and alter the balance of the shoe. Some heels are even attached to the sole with small brass tacks for added durability.

What should I know when I'm trying on shoes to make sure they're right for me?

A man can wear a pair of shoes that fit him perfectly, but if he is constantly uncertain and self-conscious about them, then that demeanor—a more unsightly display than any unsightly shoe—will show through. So it's crucial that you feel confident that the shoe style reflects your personality, and that it will be a style appropriate for where you will wear it. After you settle on the appropriate style, consider the following:

• Wear socks of the same thickness as those you will usually wear with the shoe.
• Try on shoes later in the day, after your feet expand.
• Shoes of thinner, suppler leather, such as slip-ons, stretch more than heavily built shoes, so make sure you account for this by choosing a snugly fitting shoe rather than a loosely fitting one.
• Don't let a salesperson convince you that a little breaking in, stretching or shoe cream will transform a painful shoe into a comfortable one.
• Well-fitting shoes should have creases, or break lines, straight across top of the foot.

•If a shoe feels uncomfortable even after trying them on in a number of different sizes, don't buy them.

How should I care for my shoes?

Well-made shoes will last decades if cared for properly. Consider the advice below to best prolong the life of your shoes:

•**Let them rest:** Don't wear the same shoes on consecutive days. Perspiration, absorbed into the leather when shoes are worn, needs time to air. Letting the shoe breathe for at least a day will prevent a slow rot from the inside out, and will also prevent them from smelling bad.

•**Use shoe trees:** It is crucial that shoes are stored fitted with shoe trees, preferably of cedar, which will absorb moisture, and impart a pleasant fragrance in addition to preserving the shape of the shoe. If you don't have shoe trees, stuff crumpled newspaper into your shoes.

•**Use shoe horns:** Use a shoe horn when putting on your shoes to prevent wearing away, or buckling, the back of the shoe.

•**Brush, clean and polish:** Brush off dirt after you wear your shoes and, when needed, clean them with shoe cream. "Polish them regularly with a cloth," advises Mr. Willis, of Edward Green. The cracking you might find on poorly cared for shoes is caused more from perspiration not properly dried off, than from exposure to the elements. Give them a shine with wax polish about once every three wearings. Shines do great things to leather over the years; as with an old baseball glove, the leather begins to take on a rich patina. A shine protects the leather from moisture and sun damage and retards scuffs. Some shoemakers recommend a hard, wax-based polish; others prefer the softer, fragrant bee's wax polish. Polish your shoes by first wiping them clean with a soft cloth. Then rub in polish, wax or cream with a slightly damp cloth. Wipe off the excess, let it dry, and buff with a soft-bristled brush.

•**Dry your shoes:** If you get caught in the rain, don't put your shoes near a heat source. Wipe them dry and leave them at room temperature. After a few hours, insert shoe trees to help keep their shape. Don't polish your shoes when they're wet.

•**Rejuvenate suede:** The nap of suede shoes can be renewed by softly brushing the shoes with a fine-bristled brush, or by softly rubbing them with a fine nail file.

•**Remove salt stains:** Salt, used to melt ice and snow on walk-ways, can leave unsightly white stains on shoes. Even worse, salt can do serious damage because it leeches out moisture from the leather, leaving it brittle and likely to crack. To remove salt residue (which is not visable until it sets in), first dry the shoes. If the shoes are very wet, wipe them with a dry cloth and stuff them with crumpled newspaper; if they are only slightly damp, insert shoe trees. Either way, let the shoes air out at room temperature for about an hour.

Afterward, gently rub the outside of the shoes—especially near the soles, an area where salt is most likely to lodge, and which gets the most wear-and-tear—with a cloth dampened with fresh water. This should remove most of the salt. Then, work into the leather a liberal amount of shoe cream or shoe wax. After about an hour, wipe away the excess; this should remove the remaining salt from the leather. Finally, polish the shoes as you normally do.

SOCKS

Your socks should be fun—all clothing should be fun.
                                        —Jay Kos, owner, Jay Kos Haberdashery

When you sit, climb stairs, get out of a car or step up the curb, your socks make their appearance, and when they do, you'll want them to look as smart as the rest of your attire. Many men wear only navy or black hosiery, which is safe, but dull. Why not indulge in the many attractive choices available? There are dress socks with checks, dots and argyles, to name just a few, and colors from gold to wine. Your choice of fabrics runs the gamut from cashmere to lisle cotton to merino wool to blends.

Below are some pointers on how to ensure that the space between shoe and trouser always appears impeccable.

What's the most important thing to consider when choosing socks for your wardrobe?

First, as a general rule, your socks should be darker than your suit. The darker and plainer the sock, the more conservative and dressy it is. That's why most businessmen have a collection of navy blue, black and dark-gray socks. Lighter socks command too much attention. Imagine meeting a man wearing red socks with a navy suit—his socks would be so distracting that they may be the only thing you would remember about him.

Your socks should also be roughly the same color as your shoes *or trousers*. If your socks go well with one, they'll probably go well with the other. A brown sock goes well with a tan suit and brown shoes; a navy or a black sock agrees with a navy suit and black shoes.

Second, make sure that your socks are long enough to conceal bare skin. Proper sock length ranges from mid-calf to over-the-calf. "The worst thing in the world is a short sock," says Mr. Kos, owner of New York haberdashery Jay Kos. "If you fold your leg and you're showing hair, there's something wrong."

I'm bored with wearing navy or black socks with my suit. What are some stylish options?

You can add variety to your sock wardrobe by selecting socks with different patterns and fabric weaves. While plain socks should roughly match your trousers or your shoes, any additional colors and patterns on socks should pick up, though not necessarily match, the colors of the some other item of your ensemble, such as pocket square, tie, suspenders or shirt.

Remember: the louder the color, the busier the pattern and the thicker the fabric, the more casual the sock. Wear socks of muted colors, subtle patterns and fine weaves. If the patterns are large, keep them especially subdued; a small pattern can bear a bit more color. Patterned socks should be worn with suits of a solid color or a subdued pattern, rather than with a boldly patterned suit, which might make your clothes look too busy.

PATTERNS

•**Argyle:** The argyle sock, with its sporty diamond-motif, is most commonly worn with casual clothes. Brooks Brothers claims that it became the first American retailer to manufacture argyle socks, after the company president, John Clark Wood, noticed a golfer wearing hand-knit, argyle hose and then borrowed the pattern. Jarlath Mellet, of Brooks Brothers, recommends argyles: "A guy gets a chance to do something a little bit different, plus it's still classic," he says. Although some experts say that a very subdued, finely woven argyle can look good with a suit, others maintain that argyles are too sporty for anything but casualwear.

•**Bird's Eye:** This pattern, a dense array of tiny dots (hence, the name) is a subtle addition to all suit patterns.

•**Clocks:** *Clocks* is an industry term that originally referred to silk embroidered designs on the sides of socks and stockings. Clocks are either figurative or abstract designs. For a distinguished look, choose quiet, subtle patterns.

•**Herringbone:** Small herringbone patterns in dark gray, olive or brown add texture when worn with a solid suit. Avoid wearing them with herringbone trousers; the combination will look contrived and busy.

•**Dot:** Small dots of a light color, usually on a blue or black background.

WEAVES

•**Plain:** The *plain* weave (a weave without ribbing or textures) is the most conservative-looking weave, and can be worn with nearly any suit or with casual clothes.

•**Ribbed:** *Ribbed* socks (socks woven to impart plain, raised ribs), in dark solid colors, add a textured dimension and ever-so-slight variety. The thicker the ribbing, the more casual the sock.

•**Cable:** *Cable* socks (socks woven to impart a raised rib that resembles a cable or intertwining rope) ought to be very thin when worn with business suits. They also add a sporty look and work well with casual pants and footwear. The thicker the cable, the more casual the sock.

How can I recognize well-made socks?

When you buy socks, make sure that the fabric is soft and smooth, and that the colors are clear and crisp. Find socks with a flat-across toe-seam, recommends Mr. Kalenderian, of Barneys: "The most important thing is the flat-across seam at the toe, because it won't pinch your toe," he says. Pure cotton or wool—and wool blended with nylon or cotton—are the norm in dress-sock fabrics. Wool tends to coordinate better with wool trousers, and lasts longer than cotton. In addition, fine wool socks hold to the ankle and calf better than cotton socks, which can droop and bunch. Even in a small amount, nylon will increase the life of socks. Mr. Kalenderian recommends wool blends with synthetics such as nylon, but says that synthetics should not exceed 15 percent.

How are socks sized?

Socks are sized 1 1/2 larger than shoes. For example, if your shoe size is 8, then your sock size is 9 1/2. Sock sizes range from about 9 1/2 to 13, although you may find socks sized up to 15. One-size-fits-all socks fit feet with shoe sizes from 8 1/2 to 10 1/2.

If I want to indulge, what are some luxurious fabrics?

Try socks of merino wool, cashmere, or silk-and-cashmere blends. These delicate materials will make you feel as though "you're walking on a pillow," says Joseph G. Barlow, President of New York men's clothier Harrison James. Note that cashmere wears out quickly and cashmere socks last significantly longer when blended with other fabrics, such as wool.

Which style of sock should I wear with my tuxedo?

The smoother, plainer and finer the sock, the more formal it is. Traditionally, silk socks were worn with formalwear, and they're still not a bad idea, but not necessary. When in doubt, wear black. If you're feeling confident, try a subtle pattern.

SPORT

JACKETS

The purpose of clothes, short of dandyism, is to be an impeccable backdrop to the wearer. Just a positive reinforcement of who the person is, not who the person would like to be. With real style and real taste, the clothes may be noticed, eventually, but the first image is of the entire person.

—Robert Gillotte, bespoke manager, Turnbull & Asser

The sport jacket adds versatility to your wardrobe, because it bridges your casual and dressy clothing. Indeed, both its history and its very name indicate its harmonious blend of town and country.

The prototypes of the modern sport jacket, or sport coat, were short, heavy woolen jackets created for hunting by gentlemen in 19th century England as a replacement for the longer greatcoat, the hem of which was an inconvenience when pursuing quarry on horseback or on foot. In the early decades of this century, sport jackets began to replace the suit jackets that men wore with white flannel pants at resorts.

Today, sport jackets range from traditional tweeds to blue blazers to jackets as unshaped as cardigan sweaters. Fabrics range from the original thornproof wool to linen, silk, cashmere and synthetics. Most traditional patterns—window pane, houndstooth, tweeds, herringbones, tattersalls, and so forth—evoke the countryside. But there are also dapper solid blazers and sophisticated patterns. So your options in sport coats are many.

How do suit coats and sport jackets differ?

Suit coats are meant to be worn with matching trousers, while sport jackets are not. Sport jackets are "sporty" because of their more relaxed cuts, their often bold, country-and-sport-evoking patterns and colors, and often woolly weaves. They also have sporty details, such as leather or metal buttons, patches on the elbows, pleats, patch pockets and belts.

Suit coats, with their refined silhouettes, unobtrusive details and harder fabric finishes, have a dressier look.

I sometimes wear a suit coat in place of a sport jacket. Are there guidelines on how to do this successfully?

Suit coats are similar to sport jackets but most are not similar enough to substitute for them. It's one thing to "dress up" or "dress down" an outfit through a blend of slightly different levels of attire—but mixing extremes of high and low fashion sends confusing messages. A double-breasted Savile Row suit coat would, therefore, be far too dressy to wear with non-matching trousers.

So, generally, wear your suit coats with what they were designed to be worn with: your suit trousers. An exception: the suit coat that is *unconstructed* (a coat with minimal padding and no canvas, and therefore having a soft, casual silhouette) will usually double well as a sport jacket.

What are the classic sport jackets?

The ancestor of all sport jackets probably is the Norfolk, named for the Duke of Norfolk. The Norfolk jacket allegedly was inspired by the tweed hunting suit worn by the duke. The American version of the Norfolk, created in the early 20th century, was made from the same heavy wool as the English original, with two *box pleats* (long, wide two-sided pleats that give ample room for movement) down the front and back; *bellows pockets* (pockets with deep pleats which "bellow" out for more carrying space) to accommodate shotgun cartridges; and a *bi-swing back* (a back with a lining and two deep pleats near the shoulders) for easier movement when swinging a gun. The lapel has a *storm collar* (a collar with a top button that can be fastened across the neck for warmth). The Norfolk had either no vents or two vents. A half-belt in the back was added in America to the British original.

The wools of the Norfolk and other early hunting jackets are extremely heavy, almost canvas-like, and have a high oil content which provides warmth and water resistance. "They're very functional, very long wearing, and keep you warm and dry," says Michael J. Kennelly, executive director of London's Holland & Holland, a gunmaker and sportswear outfitter. "This is the type

Norfolk Sport Jacket

of garment that a country gentleman would buy and that would be handed down. They wear like steel."

In other words, early sport jackets were fine for the life of an English squire who spent a lot of time outdoors and in drafty estate houses before the advent of central heating. But these jackets no longer are optimum indoor wear and, anyway, are a bit too countrified in cut and in material for wearing in town. Yes, the Norfolk and its cousins are classics, but, like old roadsters, perhaps not the most functional choice today. "These features—a belt, bellows—taken out of the context of the shooting world, become additional features that really have no use, so they would be less appropriate to a broader audience. The Norfolk is definitely a country jacket," says Mr. Kennelly.

Instead, try these jackets' descendants, which are made of lighter wool or cashmere, cotton, linen and a multitude of blends, and which are more comfortable and appropriate for that cocktail party or at a Sunday brunch. There's an endless variety to choose from. Double-breasted and single-breasted jackets are both classic styles, although the double-breasted is a bit dressier. Therefore, a single-breasted jacket is more versatile choice, because it can be worn with very casual clothing, such as jeans.

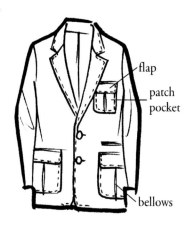

flap

patch pocket

bellows

Sport jackets, like suit jackets, are designed with one or two vents or without vents; all are equally appropriate. Mr. Kalenderian, of Barneys, believes that the casual air of the sport jacket calls for the sportiness of vents, and he prefers side vents to the less dressy single vent. "Vents add a certain elegance and style," he says. However, avoid single-vents with double-breasted sport jackets; they run counter to the dressier silhouette of the double-breasted sport jacket.

As with suits, single-breasted sport jackets with two or three-buttons are both traditional. A three-button jacket, with its longer cut, may flatter a tall men, while short men may appear engulfed.

What, exactly, is a "blazer"?

A blazer is one type of sport jacket: a jacket of a single, solid color. There are camel-hair blazers, red blazers, and, of course, the classic navy-blue blazer. According to custom suitmaker Jon Green, blazers have hard finishes while other sport jackets may not. Some historians say that the name blazer derives from late 19th century England, where their originally vibrant colors were said to "blaze."

Why are navy blazers so popular?

The blue blazer—usually made of navy-blue worsted wool—has been popular in America since the 1920s. Its popularity most likely

THE LEGEND OF THE BLUE BLAZER

According to one legend, the blue blazer got its name from its place of origin: a 19th century British Navy frigate named the *HMS Blazer*. The captain of that ship prepared for an inspection by Queen Victoria by having his crew discard their various outfits and don dark-blue jackets, of serge fabric, to spiff up their appearance. The Queen approved. The jacket endured. Indeed, it multiplied beyond the *HMS Blazer*. Today, one trace of the blazer's nautical origin remains on many makes: the brass buttons bearing the insignia of the British Navy. However, the truth of this legend is uncertain. It is also said that British sailors had worn short blue jackets since early in the 19th century, which were the prototypes for the modern blazer.

stems from its simple lines and masculine and generally flattering color; it is also among the most versatile items in a man's wardrobe, because it can be worn at casual as well as semi-formal occasions and in all seasons.

The classic navy blazer is made of *serge* wool (a smooth twill weave of worsted wool), is double-breasted (although single-breasteds have become equally standard), has side vents and brass buttons (originally with British Navy crests). These days, however, navy blue blazers come in innumerable variations and are made of fabrics ranging from cashmere to silk to linen to blends. The brass buttons now can be silver- or gold-toned. Buttons can also be of horn or plastic.

The traditional trousers worn with the blue blazer is a pair of white flannels, which were thrown on with suit coats at resorts before the blazer came along. But any gray trouser—from charcoal to the very lightest shade—is also standard.

Which sport jackets create a versatile core wardrobe?

Your core sport jacket wardrobe probably should include a navy-blue blazer, one casual jacket of a more sturdy fabric and one dressy jacket of a luxurious material. "The cornerstone of a core wardrobe would be a navy blazer, and I would complement it with one tweed and one fine lambswool or cashmere with a hard finish," advises Mr. Kennelly, of Holland & Holland.

Mr. Kalenderian suggests a core jacket wardrobe that also includes a navy serge blazer, but says that because blue blazers are so common—almost to the point of being a uniform even beyond those private schools where boys still wear them—you might want to individualize yours. You can do this a number of ways: choose a blazer with an unusual silhouette, such as one that is soft-shouldered; or consider one with distinctive details, such as a ticket pocket, or fabrics other than wool, such as cashmere. Maybe forego the blue blazer entirely, suggests Mr. Kalenderian, and find a similarly dark, plain jacket, yet one that is distinctive. "There are so many other opportunities that are more interesting and allow a person to be expressive," he says. He opts for a subtle pattern, such as a worsted lambswool *district check* (a houndstooth pattern with an overlaying check pattern) in colors such as olive-brown, navy or burgundy. "The character of these patterns is neutral, easy to coordinate, almost like a fancy solid," he says. His second jacket would be a cool-weather blazer, one of a heavy fabric, such as cashmere, and in a solid color, such as loden green, bronze or navy; or a jacket with a *caviar* pattern (a very small pattern that resembles royal oxford weave). "There are many times when people feel compelled to dress more conservatively, and this blazer is dressier than the district check," he says. His third jacket choice is one for warm weather, perhaps a cotton jacket in khaki, stone, mustard or navy.

How can I build a sport jacket wardrobe that will carry me through all seasons?

When the seasons change, so does the well-dressed man's wardrobe. Including his sport jackets. The weight of the fabric primarily determines the choice of jacket for the spring, summer, fall and winter. But colors also change.

Summer colors generally are brighter and fabric-weights are lighter than those worn in cooler weather. Warm-weather jackets are made of lightweight cotton, such as the classic cotton blue-and-white striped *seersucker* (a fabric with puckered white stripes alternating with stripes usually of light blue, green, pink or yellow). Linen is another classic warm-weather fabric, although it wrinkles easily and so has a somewhat casual look. Instead of a navy-blue wool blazer, you might, in the height of summer, try a cotton or linen blazer of a lighter shade of blue.

Worsted wool is at least a three-season fabric; if the finish is hard, and if it is medium-weight (10 ounces, for example), it can be worn in four seasons. Wool with nubby textures are better for cool weather. Cashmere is another good cool-weather fabric. Mixing wool with cashmere makes the cashmere more affordable and more durable. Other cool-weather fabrics include corduroy, flannel and moleskin. Moleskin is a traditional English fabric, sometimes called the "English denim." Hard wearing, moleskin becomes softer and more attractive the more you wear it.

The most common fabric for cold-weather sport jackets is tweed. There are a number of well-known types of tweed, including: *Harris* (generally of a heavy weight and often in herringbone) *Shetland* (typically a lighter weight than Harris, and commonly in plaids and stripes); and *Donegal* (typified by dots of color woven into the fabric).

Is it appropriate to wear a sport jacket to the office?

It depends on the atmosphere of your office. Until recently, the answer would have been that a sport jacket is too casual to serve as business attire. But informal clothing has, of course, gained increasing acceptance in business. And sport jackets are being worn more commonly. The best guide is the clothing worn by your colleagues and by the powers-that-be at your place of work. As described above, some sport jackets are dressier in appearance than others: a blue blazer or a camel hair blazer or a cashmere-and-wool double-breasted sport jacket may be more appropriate for your office than a tweed jacket.

Felix Samelson, a tailor at J. Press for more than 50 years, who fitted Frank Sinatra's Shetland wool sport jackets, notes, however, that tweed sport coats are being worn more often as a substitute for suits. "Today, in many cases, you don't have to wear the pinstripe suit. Instead, you can simply wear a nice tweed with a pair of matching slacks." With tweeds coming in lighter weights, they are easier to wear through all the seasons, he adds. Tweeds look just as distinguished with a pair of blue jeans as with gray flannel slacks and a cashmere sweater.

How can I recognize a well-made sport jacket?

"The first thing to look for is the hand of the fabric, the finish of the fabric, the purity of color, particularly in tweeds, to see the depth of the different colors—they should be clear," says Mr. Kennelly. "There should be no bumps, no loose threads. Buttons are also important to look at."

A more expensive jacket will have hand-sewn horn buttons.

Mr. Kalenderian adds that the buttons should have a shank long enough to ensure that when you button the coat, it hangs securely, yet freely.

The best sport jackets, like the best suits, are lined and have a hand-sewn canvas. More expensive jackets have canvases that are sewn, not glued to the fabric, which makes them fit better and last longer. However, Mr. Kalenderian says that "today, fusables are much softer [and] they dryclean better" than they did years ago. "If you buy a good fabric, and if it's cut right, you need not be a snob about having a canvas suit," he says.

To discern whether the canvas is fused, rub the front of the jacket near the buttons between thumb and forefinger. There should be three pieces of fabric there, with the canvas loose in between. If you feel only two pieces of fabric rubbing against one another (one of which is glued to the canvas), that's a sign that the jacket has a fused canvas.

How should a sport jacket fit?

Sport jackets fit almost the same way suit coats fit; however, winter-weight jackets may fit slightly looser than suits to accommodate a sweater or a heavy shirt worn underneath.

When you try on a jacket, prepare as you would for when you get fitted for a suit: carry any belongings that you normally would carry in the pockets: eyeglasses, wallet, keys, pens, and any other articles.

TOP OF THE LINE

Once you get at a certain price, you're paying for quality with tailored clothing. With inexpensive jackets, you can get the look of a jacket but the quality won't be there. If you want to buy a stylish jacket for a season or two, that's fine. But if you're buying it as a classic clothing investment, you're going to pay more, but it's going to last longer, because it will live through drycleaning and getting caught in the rain and it won't pucker and bubble because the canvas is sewn, not glued.

—*Michael J. Kennelly, executive director, Holland & Holland*

Again, as with suit coats, watch for the following tell-tale signs of a well-fitting jacket:

• The jacket should be long enough to cover your backside, but no longer.
• The correct jacket sleeve length extends about 1/2 inch short of a properly fitting shirt sleeve.
• Armholes should be cut high enough for free arm movement.
• Horizontal creases at the shoulders mean that the jacket is too tight; vertical creases mean that it's too loose.
• Lapels should lie flat against the chest, and flaps on pockets should drape naturally.
• The jacket collar should lie smoothly against the back of the neck, and should allow for a well-fitting shirt collar to be exposed by about 1/2 inch.

I dislike wearing a sport jacket in warm weather. Is it okay to wear a tie without a jacket?

By tradition, the necktie has belonged with the suit and, somewhat more recently, with the sport jacket. Europe's aristocracy wore neckcloths in the 17th century, using them to lend the finishing touch to their attire. Therefore, this article should not be stripped of its dignified purpose or its natural companions by wearing it over an unsheathed shirt. At any rate, to wear a necktie without a jacket is to look like an office clerk. Resist the temptation in steamy months to leave your jacket in the closet; carry your jacket over your shoulder if you must.

How should I coordinate my sport jacket with my trousers and other clothing?

• **Combining with trousers:** Whatever you do, do *not* try to match your trousers to your jacket. Remember that a sport jacket should be worn with pants that don't match. And avoid wearing them with most suit trousers, which will usually appear to be exactly what they are. Sport coats can either be lighter or darker than the trousers they are worn with. The classic combination with a blue blazer, for example, is white or gray flannel trousers.

But while you don't want to perfectly match pants to your jacket, that doesn't mean you should hop into the first pair you happen to grab from your closet. You want jacket and trouser to play off each other well, or *complement*, each other. That means you should think of two things when you mate jacket with trousers: fabric and color. Select trousers of fabric that is similar in character and weight to that of your jacket. For example, a heavy Donegal tweed jacket demands a hefty trouser. The fabric needn't be the same, though; pants of substantial cotton, such as moleskin or corduroy, work well with thick wool jackets. Again, the goal is to coordinate jacket and trouser fabrics by weight and by the roughness or smoothness of the weave—not the precise type of fabric.

Trouser cuffs are a bit dressier than plain-leg, but the choice is yours. Both are correct with sport jackets.

Be careful about wearing patterned trousers with a patterned jacket. Don't create a battlefield for your patterns unless you want to elicit giggles or scorn. So keep your pants plain if your jacket is busy. Or at least keep the patterns at different sizes and at different levels of boldness.

•**Combining with shirts:** Your shirt and sport jacket should play off one another well. For example, if you're wearing a jacket with big, bright, canary-colored window panes, then keep the pattern of your shirt small and discreet. And the patterns' colors, of course, should subtly echo one another.

•**Combining with ties:** Your tie choice for a heavy sport jacket would be a tie with a substantial hand—perhaps a tie of wool, cashmere or thickly-woven silk. This approach holds for pocket squares: go for a wool or cashmere or a blend, in order to correlate the weight of the fabric to the texture of the pocket square. A nubby tweed jacket contrasts too much with a pocket square of fine silk or a handkerchief of stiff cotton or linen, which would go better with lighter, summer sport jackets or blazers of tropical wool, linen or cotton, for example.

As always, don't precisely match your handkerchief with your tie: one of the most important things in wearing pocket squares with sport jackets is color palette: work with a palette that is either complementary or contrasting.

•**Combining with shoes and belts:** Lastly, as for shoes and belts: they should be a bit casual yet still dressy, in keeping with the sport jacket's stylish casualness.

OUTERWEAR

Overcoats give a first, and lasting, impression.
—Stephen Milstein, vice president, Burlington Coat Factory

A well-fitting coat is a sign of success.
—Christopher Pendleton, CEO, Aquascutum

You may consider an overcoat a merely utilitarian item, meant only to protect your suit and keep you warm. But because your overcoat conceals the rest of your clothes, it can be the defining image that others have of you—whether you're walking along a city street, or entering an office lobby or a four-star restaurant. A coat that has an unflattering style, that fits poorly, or that appears cheaply made can kill an otherwise strong look.

Dressy overcoats, such as the Chesterfield, derive from the 19th century frock coat. Casual overcoats and some raincoats were originally military coats, and some vestigial details persist, such as epaulets, belts, peaked lapels, double-breasted fronts. The trench coat, for example, was developed by Burberrys for British soldiers during World War I.

Through the decades, overcoat lengths have ranged from above the knee to the trouser bottoms; silhouettes have ranged from the close-fitting to great, flowing expanses of cloth, usually adapting to the changing silhouettes of suits. However, some elements of overcoats have remained constant: suit-like lapels, single- or double-breasted fronts and single vents.

A number of classic styles are described in this chapter; however, you will frequently encounter coats that have a mingling of styles. Those coats that are closest to the classics will provide enduring style and the most versatility.

How do topcoats, overcoats and raincoats differ?
These days, the terms topcoat and overcoat are used as synonyms, but there are differences between the two. Traditionally, topcoats were designed for wearing over suits and dinner jackets in spring

and summer, while overcoats were meant for winter wear. Top-coats are made of fabric weights of about 12 ounces per square yard; overcoats by contrast, are made of fabrics of weights of about 14 ounces per square yard and heavier. Overcoats are made of heavy wools, such as tweeds, and other substantial but dressy fabrics, such as cashmere, camel hair, *Angora* (fabric made from hair of the Angora goat) and mohair (fabric made from from Angora mixed with other fibers, such as cotton). Overcoats are typically longer than topcoats.

Raincoats differ from both topcoats and overcoats in that they are not only a more recent innovation, becoming popular only in the 20th century, but are also made of different materials: light-weight, water-resistant or waterproof fabrics (such as chemically treated cottons). They usually have a removable lining.

What are the classic overcoat styles?

There are several classic overcoat styles. You'll probably find in clothing shops that certain overcoats may be modified versions of the classic styles described below. Stephen Milstein, vice president of Burlington Coat Factory, says: "In the case of overcoats, you may see modifications of the classic models, like at the length of the coats or the width of the lapel, but in most overcoats, usually 80 percent of the [classic, original] style remains intact."

•**Balmacaan:** The Balmacaan is distinguished by its short collar. It is single-breasted, has a *fly-front* (a front with concealed buttons), and has a generous silhouette. Its sleeves are in the *raglan* style (sleeves attached at the collar instead of at the shoulder points). Usually, the Balmacaan is made in tan or navy.

•**British Warm:** The British warm is a double-breasted, peaked-lapel, knee-length overcoat. Epaulets on the shoulder give it a military air.

It was traditionally made in "British pink," a grayish taupe wool, according to Mr. Milstein. It is also made in dark wools, camel hair, and cavalry twill (an extra-heavy, tear-resistant twill weave).

•**Chesterfield:** Named after the Earl of Chesterfield, a fashionable aristocrat of the Victorian age, the chesterfield is the dressiest of overcoats. The chesterfield is distinguished by short lapels, the upper part of which

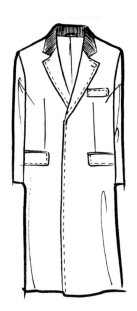

is traditionally of black or brown velvet, in contrast with a lighter toned coat fabric. Usually the fabric is herringbone, dark gray, navy blue, or *covert* wool (a twill wool of slightly different hues of the same color, usually mossy green).

The classic chesterfield is the single-breasted, which usually has a fly front and *set-in* sleeves (sleeves that are cut vertically at the shoulder points, like those of a suit coat).

The double-breasted version has exposed buttons.

"There isn't anything more dressy or elegant than a dark-gray herringbone chesterfield coat with a velvet collar," says Mr. Pendleton, CEO of London clothier Aquascutum.

•**Polo:** The classic collegiate coat, the polo became popular after Brooks Brothers introduced it to the United States from Britain in 1910. According to Brooks Brothers, the polo was originally white with pearl buttons and only later was made of camel hair. American Ivy Leaguers adopted the style from British polo players who had come to the States for polo matches, and who, it is said, wore these coats between playing periods. The polo coat is cut below the knee and usually has patched, flap pockets at the hips and a half-belt in back. It has a full cut, is usually double-breasted and has set-in sleeves. With sporty details (such as the

half-belt) and a somewhat dressy cut, the polo is adaptable to both casualwear and businesswear. Traditionally made of pure camel hair, the polo is also made of cashmere, lambswool or blends. Note that camel hair, which is extremely soft, wears out quickly, so that blends may be desirable.

•**Trench:** Burberrys of London claims to have created this raincoat for British troops to keep them dry in the trenches during World War I. The trench coat, despite its military, rather than dressy appearance, has since become a staple in the businessman's wardrobe. In its classic form, the trench coat has a fairly relaxed fit, very wide lapels, and busy, military-style details such as epaulets, straps on the wrists and a loose belt.

J. Stanley Tucker, senior vice president of Burberrys, says that the trench coat originally was a double-breasted cotton gabardine and, while this remains the template for modern trench coats, it now comes in many variations. "Most people think of the trench coat as a raincoat, because it was originally meant to be water resistant, but it has since evolved into all kinds of fabrications," says Mr. Tucker. Trench coats are made in single- and double-breasted styles; most have a button-out or zip-out lining, for all-season wear.

•**Wrap:** The wrap is distinguished by its robe-like silhouette, formed by a long, loose belt that wraps the front fabric across to one side. This coat is roomy and has a casual drape, and so it should not be worn over dressy suits or formalwear.

•**Duffel:** The duffel is a casual coat, and is distinguished by wooden or horn *toggle* buttons (peg-like buttons), leather button loops and a heavy hood. The duffel coat usually is made of thick wool of tan or navy.

•**Car Coat:** The car coat includes any coat of a mid-thigh length (about 34 to 36 inches), which makes these coats less bulky when you're seated in a car. Generally, a casual coat.

•**Loden Coat:** Strictly speaking, the loden is an overcoat made of *loden* wool (heavy, forest-green wool from Tyrol, Austria). Traditionally, the coat was cut at the mid-thigh, but it is now commonly worn well below the knee. The collar is usually short, resembling a shirt collar. The silhouette flows from a fitted chest to a broad skirt. In Europe, this coat, despite its somewhat sporty cut, is often worn over suits as well as over casual clothing.

•**Single-Breasted and Double-Breasted Overcoats:** This broad category includes all other overcoats that are single-breasted or double-breasted. Single-breasteds have notched lapels and double-breasteds have peaked lapels. These coats are typically full-length (the average overcoat is about 48 inches long) with *button-through fronts* (the buttons fasten through the front of the jacket and are visable, as opposed to the fly-front, which conceals the buttons). They have a single rear vent, and flap pockets or *slash* pockets (pockets without flaps, cut at an angle). They are made of fabrics such as cashmere, camel hair, tweed, angora or plain-weave wool, and are commonly navy blue, gray, tan and black.

Single-breasted   *Double-breasted*

How can I determine the best overcoat style for me?

Here, the issues are: double- or single-breasted? Set-in or raglan sleeves? Belted or not? How long? What color? Which type of fabric? Mr. Tucker, of Burberrys, suggests that the answers to these questions depend on your height, and whether you frequently wear suits or more casual clothes.

Your height should "dictate whether you buy a single- or double-breasted," advises Mr. Tucker. A double-breasted coat, like a double-breasted suit, will make a short man look even shorter, according to Mr. Tucker. Short men also should avoid very long overcoats, which detract from height. He also recommends for short men a coat with a belt, which narrows the silhouette and "brings your eye up to the waist."

Next, says Mr. Tucker, determine whether you'd prefer the coat to have set-in or raglan sleeves. (Aquascutum claims to have invented the raglan sleeve for Britain's one-armed Lord Raglan "to give him freedom of movement whilst making a mess of the charge of the Light Brigade.")

Overcoats with set-in sleeves are, as a rule, cut closer to the body than raglans, and generally are designed to resemble a suit by the cut of their lapels, use of patch hip-pockets and other details.

Raglan coats, which have a looser drape, are generally sporty, with details such as banded sleeve-cuffs, the more casual slash pockets, and a flairing skirt. "A casual coat is going to be looser, will have a more boxy fit, whereas a dressier coat, such as the chesterfield, will be much more fitted-looking," says Mr. Tucker.

The raglan works well with casual clothes as well as with most suits, and so is the more versatile of the two styles: "It's more comfortable, and it's more serviceable because you can wear it with sportswear as well as with dress wear and get away with it," says Mr. Tucker.

But a man who wears suits regularly, especially suits with very padded shoulders, may prefer a coat with set-in sleeves. "If you wear a suit with built-up shoulders under a raglan-sleeve coat, it won't look very nice," says Mr. Tucker, because the square, padded shoulder will bulge against the coat's drapey shoulder fabric.

For decades, wearing an overcoat with casualwear has been fashionable on university campuses and, as clothing becomes more casual everywhere, it is increasingly common to see overcoats worn without suits or sport jackets underneath. But if you don't wear a jacket, then it's best to be cautious about wearing an overcoat with set-in sleeves. As explained above, a coat with set-in sleeves is

Raglan Sleeve   *Set-in Sleeve*

a dressy, square-shouldered, tailored style, and it is designed to be worn over a suit. So you may be mixing casual and dressy in a way that won't work.

What's a good core overcoat wardrobe?

Experts recommend that a man own a raincoat and at least one dark overcoat. But your core overcoat wardrobe should reflect your lifestyle. As with suits, the most common overcoat colors are navy and gray, with brown considered more countrified and casual. A man who lives in a cold climate and works in a traditional profession, may find a dark wool overcoat best. A man who lives in a warmer region may be best off with a light-weight, and perhaps shorter, overcoat or topcoat.

Is it improper to wear a short, casual coat with my suit?

Some casual coats have been dressed up with more expensive fabrics and lengthened to serve as an overcoat. These may include the *pea coat* (a short, navy-blue wool jacket with wide, peaked lapels), the duffel or even the *Mackinaw* (a coat cut just below waist, usually of heavy plaid wool). These are handsome coats, and are increasingly used as overcoats, though seldom in conservative professions. Europeans have embraced the shorter, three-quar-

THE CORE OVERCOAT WARDROBE

For pure functionality, I would first buy a raincoat with a zip-out or button-out lining, which would serve one from the spring through winter, and it is acceptable in inclement as well as sunny weather. Then, I'd recommend a shorter length coat—a car-coat length—in wool, blended with cashmere or camel hair. This can be worn both on weekends and over a suit. The most versatile color would be navy blue. I would stay away from brown, but if you want, wear it during the daytime with a suit.

—J. Stanley Tucker, senior vice president, Burberrys

The most versatile overcoat would be a single-breasted overcoat in wool or cashmere. This model would accommodate sports coats and would be appropriate with a tuxedo as well. As for color choices, navy is the most versatile, although the traditional camel hair is acceptable in almost every situation. Today, however, more casual styles are gaining popularity. Three-quarter-length coats in better wool fabrics that can be worn over suits, but that can also serve as weekend coats over sportswear, are also gaining acceptance.

—Charles McGlothlin, general manager and buyer, Faconnable

I would say your first coat should be navy blue, because it can be dressy, it can be casual, and it can be worn in the day and into evening. Navy goes with anything—it goes well over gray and it's more fashionable than brown or tan. A second choice would be gray. I would look for something that has a little cashmere in it, considering that you may not want to spend the extra for a pure cashmere coat. Just fifteen percent of cashmere makes all the difference in the world, in the lightness of it and the softness of it. As for style, I would say the best all-occassion coat is a raglan, because it can be dressy, it can be casual, you can wear it with a pair of corduroys and a sweater or you can wear it over a gray flannel suit. A coat with set-in sleeves looks funny with casual clothes. Length should definitely be below the knee. A good second coat would be a plain raincoat with a button-out lining. It's a waste of money to buy an unlined raincoat.

—Christopher Pendleton, CEO, Aquascutum

ter-length coats worn just above the knee as overcoats. Also, synthetic *micro-fibers* (extremely fine synthetic fibers which produce a suede-like nap) in bolder colors are more popular in Europe and in some of the more sartorially relaxed regions of the United States.

The convergence of the casual weekend coat and the traditional full-length overcoat may be a response by designers to the strengthening trend toward dressed-up casual clothing. Just make sure that your coat is longer than your suit coat.

Is using a raincoat as an overcoat inappropriate?

Of course, on rainy days, raincoats are fine with suits. But they shouldn't be used as a permanent replacement for an overcoat—better to own a raincoat in addition to a dark wool overcoat. If an overcoat is too warm for the weather, try a topcoat. "Clearly, wearing a topcoat makes you better dressed," says Walter B.D. Hickey, Jr., chairman of Hickey-Freeman. "Some men use a raincoat through the summer and think they can just put the lining in for colder weather, and they'll have a sufficient topcoat. This really isn't how a well-dressed man approaches things," he says.

What's the right overcoat for black-tie affairs?

The chesterfield with velvet collar is a classic coat for black tie. Single- and double-breasted overcoats in black cashmere or wool are also traditionally worn over formalwear. Keep in mind that overcoats with belts, wrist bands and raglan sleeves are details of a casual coat. Never wear a raincoat with a tuxedo. "At every formal event you inevitably see men entering wearing the usual wrinkled raincoat and frantically looking for the coat check. It is evident they don't quite look correct, and are looking to unload the offending culprit," says Charles McGlothlin, general manager and buyer of Facconable, the Paris-based men's clothier. "If you can possibly make the investment, nothing completes the look better or makes you feel better than a great topcoat."

How can I recognize a well-made overcoat?

"First, touch the coat," Mr. Tucker recommends. "One of the most important elements in discerning quality is the fabric. The second thing to look at is the quality of stitching, which should be strong and secure, with no loose threads. Construction is critical for a well-made garment—look for bemberg [a high-quality, silk-like rayon] linings, horn buttons, stitching that is even and straight." Mr. Pendleton, of Aquascutum, agrees, adding: "Look at the quality of the buttons to determine whether they are made of good horn." You can tell a good horn button because it has a "coloration that is not uniform and it's not shiny," he says.

Like most suits, few overcoats have hand-sewn canvases "unless you get into the $2,000 and up category," says Mr. Pendleton. But he says that "fusing has developed to a level by the better manufacturers where some things are done better by machines than by hand. A real traditionalist would disagree with that."

How can I get the best possible fit?

Your overcoat should be large enough to protect you and your suit from the elements, but it also should not overwhelm you. And of course, it shouldn't be too snug (watch for pulling of fabric at the shoulder blades and at the seat and chest). Below are some further points to consider when trying on an overcoat:

• **Chest and Collar:** The most noticed areas of your overcoat are the chest and collar because they are closest to your face, says Mr. Pendleton. Therefore, it's crucial that your overcoat fits well in those places. Make sure your coat collar (like your suit collar) is snug against your neck and that it is high enough to cover your shirt collar.

• **Sleeves:** Overcoat sleeves should be long enough to cover the sleeves of your suit and shirt, which means that your coat sleeves should be about 1/2 inch longer than your suit sleeves. Any shorter and you'll reveal your shirt cuffs; any longer and your overcoat sleeves will drape over your hands.

• **Upper Body:** For a correct fit around the upper body, be sure to wear a suit coat or sport jacket and, perhaps, a sweater, when you try on the overcoat.

•**Silhouette:** Check the overcoat's silhouette with the same attention that you would when you try on a suit. Make sure the fabric doesn't bulge or flare, especially in the backside area.

•**Length:** Traditionally, an overcoat is long enough to cover the knees, but not so long that it will restrict one when walking. The optimum length is between just below the knee to half-way down the calf. If the coat's skirt is above the knee, some experts say it will make the upper body appear too large in proportion to the lower body. If it's too long, it will hinder you.

•**Vents:** A single vent should be high enough to accomodate unfettered movement, but not so high that it leaves you unprotected from the elements.

ACCESSORIES

It's really the accessory, such as braces, that punctuates the statement of a man's style.

—Michele Toia, designer, Trafalgar Ltd.

The expression of accessories is very personal.

—Tom Kalenderian, executive vice president, men's merchandizing, Barneys New York

Accessories differ from suits, shoes, shirts and other clothing, because they are meant primarily to express the wearer's personality. Accessories include that cognac-hued alligator-skin belt; that Irish linen handkerchief; that natty Montecristi Panama hat; those Japanese-silk suspenders. They range from the obscene to the sublime, from the exquisite to the dime-a-dozen. Some accessories, such as cuff links, once were essential parts of a man's wardrobe but have become obsolete, and now endure solely because they add a finishing touch to a man's attire. Other items, such as the breastpocket handkerchief, have always been purely ornamental. It is wise to choose classic accessories, which contribute panache and, sometimes, tasteful humor to an outfit.

SUSPENDERS AND BELTS

Is there a difference between "suspenders" and "braces"?
The British call these 18th century contraptions that hold up a man's trousers *braces* and Americans refer to them as *suspenders*. But the terms are interchangable and the styles and construction are the same on both sides of the Atlantic.

I'm considering buying suspenders. What are my choices?
Your choices are as endless as your choices of ties because suspenders' fabric, called the *webbing*, comes in the same patterns as ties—rep, dot, club, etc.—and in as many hues. The webbing is most commonly made of nylon (first used for suspenders in the late 1940s). But better suspenders are made of silk, of the same qual-

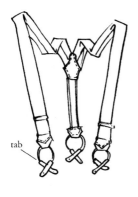

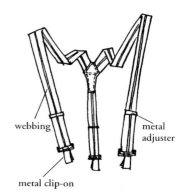

Tab Suspenders   *Clip-on Suspenders*

ity as tie silk. Other good, though less common, suspender-web-bings include those made of wool, silk-and-wool, silk-and-linen or felt. Patterns may be woven, like tie patterns, into the fabric or they may be printed onto the fabric, a cheaper method. However, printed patterns are not necessarily worse than a woven webbing, if the style is flattering. The *tabs* (or *ends*) of suspenders, which fasten to the trouser waistband, are made of rayon, braided silk, string covered with silk, cat gut (a rarity), or of a variety of leathers, which may be flat or curved. Superior suspenders have ends of high-quality calfskin or goatskin. The metal *levers* (also called *adjusters*) are finished with brass, nickle or other metals.

Are button-on suspenders a better choice than clip-ons?

According to conventional wisdom, clip-on suspenders are less elegant than those that button on to trousers. Men buy button-ons because they are "a reflection of their personality, rather than to simply hold up their trousers," says Michele Toia, a designer at Trafalgar. New York clothier Jay Kos puts it more pointedly: "It looks horrible to wear clip-ons. They're not clean. If you're a farmer, it's okay." Some suspenders are equipped with both styles of tabs, so you can alternate.

Which are preferable, belts or suspenders?

Note here the operative word is *or*: never wear both a belt and suspenders at the same time. There's no need to. It's redundant.

Some history: Early in this century, dressy trousers rarely had belt loops. Belts were worn by blue-collar workers while suspenders were worn with business and formal attire. However, few would even know that a man was wearing suspenders, which were considered an undergarment to be kept concealed beneath the ubiquitous vest.

After World War I, belts gained in popularity and through the decades increasingly replaced suspenders. In the 1980s, suspenders became fashionable again, especially on Wall Street, and the fashion spread through the United States. They have remained widely worn.

Today, Americans' collective memories no longer associate belts with laborers. And we no longer consider suspenders as undergarments meant to be hidden—indeed they are considered a dressy touch.

A belt is as appropriate as suspenders for wearing with a suit or sport jacket, although suspenders remain the only choice for black tie or white tie. Aside from the advice that you should not wear belts and suspenders together, there are only two additional aesthetic points to keep in mind: first, don't wear a belt if you wear a vest: a belt creates a bulge, and a buckle ruins the look of simplicity of a vest and trousers. Second, you should wear a tie if you wear suspenders because a four-in-hand provides aesthetic balance by adding to the vertical suspender lines, and helps create the dressier look that suspenders have come to convey. A bow tie also spiffs up a man's appearance when he wears suspenders.

As for which is preferable—a belt or suspenders—it is solely a matter of personal taste. Both belts and suspenders have benefits and drawbacks. Suspenders advocates praise these shoulder straps for allowing trousers to drape at their most flattering; holding trousers in place at the waist from above, so they don't slip to the hip; permitting your waistband to expand when when you sit, unlike belts; and preventing the waistband fabric from bunching up. Furthermore, suspenders emphasize the verticality of the body, while belts emphasize the horizontal. On the other hand, belt advocates argue that suspenders can slip off sloping shoulders, are warm against the body in summer and are an affectation.

Is there any occasion that demands that I wear a belt instead of suspenders?

Always wear a belt if you are not wearing suspenders, except when you are wearing formal attire. Trousers with empty belt loops present an unfinished appearance.

What's the proper way to wear suspenders?

Two aspects require your attention: the metal adjusters and the buttons. The adjusters, which draw attention because they are brass or some other shiny metal, should rest at the middle area of your torso, neither too close to your face, nor too close to your trouser waistband.

On the front of your trousers, suspenders connect to two pairs of buttons stitched inside the waistband on either side of the fly. One button of each pair should aligned with the largest pleat (the one that becomes the trouser's crease). The other button is located closer to the side pocket.

In the back of your trousers, there typically are two buttons for your suspenders: one on either side of the center. Suspender buttons were once placed on the outside, rather than the inside, of trousers, but nearly all buttons today are on the inside.

If your trousers don't have buttons for suspenders, you can ask a tailor to sew them on.

How should I coordinate my suspenders with the rest of my attire?

Your suspenders' colors and patterns primarily should complement, but not perfectly match, those of your tie, and secondarily those of your shirt and trousers. "But you don't want them to match," says Mr. Kos. "Because it will look ridiculous. A well-dressed person's clothes look a little unplanned."

Don't worry about coordinating your suspenders with your suit or sport jacket, because suspenders will be seen only when your jacket is removed.

To coordinate your suspenders with your tie, keep the colors of your suspenders *similar* to at least one of the colors of your tie. "We suggest that the brace complement one of the accent colors in the tie—not the dominant color," says Ms. Toia, of Trafalgar.

To avoid the matchy look, keep the designs of your tie and suspenders different. If you're wearing a blue-and-gold striped tie, for example, don't wear striped suspenders; instead, try solid or checkered webbings. Or strap on plaid-patterned suspenders.

Ms. Toia recommends solid burgundy because it is the most versatile color for suspenders; it works well with an array of colors, such as navy, white and gray. But Ms. Toia also notes that there are many adventurous styles, too, including "conversational" suspenders, with sport-and-leisure motifs ranging from golfers to matadors-and-bulls. "Wearing braces can be a happy blend of classic good taste with a bit of eccentricity and a dash of humor," says Ms. Toia.

Is it okay to wear a button-down collar with suspenders?

Yes, but wear that button-down with a bow tie or a four-in-hand.

How can I recognize well-made suspenders?

First, check the quality of the fabric, advises Ms. Toia. Whatever the suspenders are made of—silk, felt, nylon or any other fabric—that fabric should have a fine feel and look. As with ties, patterns that are woven into the fabric are considered more elegant than those that are printed on. And, whether woven or printed, the

SUSPENDERS
30-SECOND QUALITY TEST

•**Fabric:** The quality of the webbing fabric should be superior; printed patterns should be clean and clear. The webbing should be about 1 1/2 inches wide, to provide comfort.

•**Tabs:** The leather of the tabs should be supple; stitching on the tabs should be discreet.

•**Adjusters:** The finish on the metal adjusters should be flawless.

pattern should be clear and crisp.

If the tabs are of leather, the leather should be supple, and the stitching discreet, which imparts a dressier look than bolder stitching. Curved ends add some richness.

The finish on the adjusters should be clean.

The webbing should be about an 1 1/2 inches wide at the shoulder. If suspenders are too narrow, they'll cause discomfort.

What's the most important thing I should consider when shopping for a belt?

You should own belts of black, brown and cordovan, selected to roughly match the color of your shoes. Your belt should be darker than your suit and long enough to buckle into the second hole (or, the belt tip should extend through the first belt loop). This usually means buying a belt sized a bit larger than your trouser waist size, because belts are sized smaller than trousers. Dressy belts should be no more than 1 1/2 inches wide.

Make sure your belts are of high-quality leather, such as calfskin. Alligator skin, lizard skin and snakeskin add interesting textures. The buckle on dress belts should not be large or flashy, because it will draw attention to your stomach. Casual belts can be wider, lighter in color, made of canvas or other fabrics, and with showier and larger buckles.

How should I care for my belt?

Give your belts a full lifespan by periodically rubbing them with a clear leather-polish. Clear polish will keep the leather supple, conceal wear-and-tear, and won't stain your trousers. As for storage: hang your belts from the buckle.

POCKET HANDKERCHIEFS

I don't wear a handkerchief in the breast pocket of my jacket. Should I?

There are many reasons why you should. A handkerchief spiffs up any jacket instantly and inexpensively and makes a fine suit or sport jacket look even finer. It also makes a not-so-good jacket, or one that is threadbare, look, well, less so. Yes, fewer men wear them these days, to the point that some say they have a look of old-fashioned elegance. Perhaps that's true; handkerchiefs and squares date back at least to the early 19th century in England as a breast-pocket adornment. They became widely popular among men in the 1920s but declined in use during the 1960s. Since the 1980s, however, they have made a resurgence. And they remain a classic accessory to a man's wardrobe.

What is the difference between a pocket square and a pocket handkerchief?

A pocket *handkerchief* is a cloth woven of white linen or white cotton. A *pocket square* usually is of silk, but a square also includes silk blends, cashmere, wool and other fine fabrics. A pocket handkerchief, properly worn, has a crisp appearance, with a few sharp corner-points visible from the top of the jacket breast-pocket, or with a neat, horizontal plane of white showing. In 19th century England, linen handkerchiefs were the choice of the upper classes, while the cheaper cotton handkerchiefs were used by working class men. The white linen handkerchief is still considered the finer of

the two, and remains the most traditional breast pocket adornment. The silk square has a softer look, and so is displayed in a
puff (a swell of fabric) that overflows from the pocket. Squares are
offered in solids and in the same patterns that ties are: foulard,
dot, stripe, club, paisleys, geometrics, and many others. Handkerchiefs and squares come in the same sizes: 13 1/2 to 17 1/2 square
inches (35 to 45 square centimeters). Because the term "handkerchief" also once defined a pocket square, we use that term to
include both, for convenience, unless specifically referring to a
pocket square.

How should I combine my handkerchief with the rest of my attire?

The handkerchief's colors, design and fabric-weight primarily should
coordinate with those of your tie, but your handkerchief also should
be friendly with your jacket and your shirt. As with suspenders,
the most important principle of successfully mating handkerchiefs
with your tie is: don't match them precisely. There have been
brief periods, such as the early 1940s, when American men tended
to match tie and handkerchief, but most well-dressed men through
the decades have felt that perfectly matched handkerchiefs and ties
strip a man's attire of spontaneity and impose the rigid look of a
parade-ground uniform. "You don't want to match it so precisely;
express your individuality with insouciance," urges Mr.
Kalenderian, of Barneys.

To coordinate your handkerchief and tie (and you *should* wear
a tie because an empty collar contradicts the dressy look of the
handkerchief) wear a handkerchief that picks up any of the tie's
colors and that is of a slightly different design than the tie (or
shirt), again to avoid the matchy look. If your tie (or shirt) is colorful and busy, then wear a muted handkerchief, and vice-versa. Also,
try to coordinate the weight of the fabric of your handkerchief to
that of your tie and jacket. A tweed jacket, for example, with its
nubby, countrified look, is best worn with a heavier, more casual
pocket square of, say, wool or cashmere. A starched, white linen
handkerchief would appear too flimsy and formal with such a

jacket. It would, however, go nicely with a linen or cotton summer suit, or with any suit, for that matter. "A white handkerchief is very often worn with suits because it certainly conveys a corporate look," says Mr. Kalenderian.

Also, make sure a linen or cotton handkerchief's edges have a good *roll* (a slightly raised edge) which adds a decorative effect. Bright, bold handkerchiefs bring gaity to your wardrobe; darker ones lend you an air of seriousness.

Your pocket handkerchief is meant for show. Keep another, plain white cotton handkerchief in your trouser pocket for use.

When I wear a pocket handkerchief, am I also supposed to wear a tie?

It's better to wear a tie with a pocket handkerchief. Even if you don't wear a tie, a handkerchief adds flair to casual attire.

How many handkerchiefs should a well-dressed man own?

Own at least one white handkerchief, of linen, or cotton as a second best. They are dressy yet versatile, and for decades have been *the* standard breast-pocket embellishments. You also might want a few handkerchiefs or pocket squares with some navy, burgundy or gray in them, which are among the most adaptable colors. Note that silk pocket squares, with their luxurious sheen, may be perceived by some as foppish.

How is a handkerchief properly displayed?

Remember the distinction between a handkerchief and a pocket square: a handkerchief is meant to look crisp, and so is folded, in order to present from one to four *points* (stiff corners) above the breast pocket. Silk squares, however, which are woven of softer material than cotton, are meant to be tucked gently into your breast pocket, and the middle of the fabric should swell above the top in a puff. Note that it's perfectly okay to wear a handkerchief if the breast pocket is partially blocked by the the coat lapel.

The following are four methods of folding your handkerchief:

•**Multi-pointed:** This style has two to four points. Some say it appears too contrived:

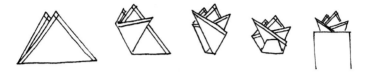

•**Triangle Fold:** A modest, yet elegant style for men who want just a hint of handkerchief to show:

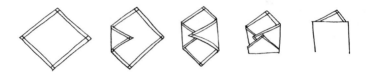

•**TV Fold:** Yet another way to display your handkerchief is to abandon the points altogether and fold it so that it peeks out in a horizontal strip about 1/2 inch above the breast pocket. This subdued style is known as the *TV fold,* because it was popular among television entertainers in the 1940s and 1950s. Its inconspicuous appearance may be most comfortable for some first-time handkerchief wearers.

One way to wear a handkerchief without folding it: tamp it casually in your jacket breast pocket with a few of the points jutting up an inch or so. Give an appearance of casualness, not meticulousness. To best achieve this casual look, simply press the center of the handkerchief through your thumb and forefinger, then stuff it in your pocket.

Whether it's woven of linen, cotton or silk, the cloth of your handkerchief should rise no more than about 1 1/2 inches from your breast pocket. Much less and it gets lost. "For somebody who is a bit more flamboyant," suggests Paul Stuart, "he might want to show a lot more pocket square; for somebody who is conservative, he might show less."

Try angling your handkerchief so it rises a bit higher outward, toward the left shoulder, which emphasizes the shoulder's width and adds a jaunty touch.

CUFF LINKS

When should a man wear cuff links?

Since the 19th century, when cuff links became widely used, they have been commonly worn with business suits and with formal attire. However, with fashion trending more casual, some fashion experts suggest that cuff links may be appropriately worn with a sport jacket and even without a tie.

Cuff links were traditionally connected by a small chain (today, called *chain links*), and were usually made of black onyx, a stone that remains a popular choice for daywear. Other standard cuff links are those made of gold, silver, enamel or mother-of-pearl.

You still *must* wear cufflinks when you wear a tuxedo, and you should wear them with matching shirt studs. Black onyx cuff links are appropriate for formalwear and for business attire. Other stones, such as emeralds, also can be tastefully worn with black tie attire, although they may be a bit flashy for businesswear. Mother-of-pearl cuff links are most appropriate for white tie.

What are the classic cuff links?

Although there are no "classic" patterns or images, there are a few classic shapes of cuff links. *Double-faced* cuff links (links with two identical faces) are perhaps the most elegant. They and *pushthroughs* (links with bulbous ends) are preferable to non-matched links, known as *hinged-back* (links with a bar on the inside), because the bar, rather than the decorative face, is seen on the inside of your cuff. *Silk knots* are acceptable, but they aren't quite as dressy as cuff links made of metals or of stones. There are also cuff links that snap together, which date back to the first decades of this century.

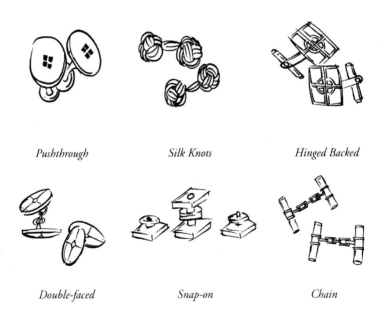

Pushthrough	Silk Knots	Hinged Backed
Double-faced	*Snap-on*	*Chain*

What about other jewelry?

In some places, in some periods of history, men's fashion has veered toward the baroque. Gold rings. Jeweled necklaces. Frilled lace. Feathered hats. Velvet jackets. But since the early 19th century, simplicity and somber colors have dominated men's clothing. Jewelry, no doubt, will come back in fashion, as it did briefly in the 1960s. But these days, while some men wear a lot of jewelry—pinky rings, chest medallions, bracelets, and so forth—most men don't. Especially in traditional professions.

What are the most important things I should look for when shopping for cuff links?

Cuff links are one of the few accessories that may be chosen solely for their own appeal; they need not be coordinated with any other article of clothing. Some men do choose to match their cuff links with their watch and ring, however, by keeping all jewelry of either gold or silver, for example. But with cuff links, anything goes. There are no traditional patterns or designs. Double ovals of enamel, gold or silver, however, have long been a common style. Just make sure that your cuff links aren't too large or garish, in keeping with the rest of your dressy or formal attire.

COLLAR BARS

Why do some men wear a collar bar? Is it more correct, or traditional, to wear one?

Collar bars first appeared around 1900 as a way to pull together the points of the collar and provide an outward thrust for the tie knot. Collar bars provide a tidy, dressy look, and one that, these days, *may* appear a bit old-fashioned and fussy, particularly on a young man. They're a rarity now, but they're still worn. If you like collar bars, make sure they're not flashy—avoid bars with emeralds or other jewelry. Most commonly, collar bars are made in a *safety-pin* style, or a simple *straight bar*. And wear them only with a suit: they're a bit too dressy for a sport jacket. Another option: wear a tab collar, which serves the same purpose as a collar bar but without the flash and they're more adaptable to a sport jacket.

Are special collars necessary for collar bars?

Wear collar bars with straight-point collars or rounded collars. But don't wear collar bars with wide spread-collars: they cancel each other out (one pulls together, the other extends sideways). You can probably find collars with holes for collar bars. But shirts of high-quality cotton won't be damaged by the holes, which will close when the shirt is laundered.

TIE CLIPS AND TIE PINS

Tie clips and tie pins seem antiquated. Are they generally seen that way these days?

Yes, tie clips and tie pins, like collar bars, no longer are commonly worn, and are especially rare among men under, say, forty. They do, however, serve to keep your tie in place if, like most men, you don't wear a vest. If you don't find any contempory clips or pins that appeal to you, try antique styles.

I don't like throwing my tie over my shoulder while I eat to avoid food stains. Would a tie clip or tie pin help?

Yes, you could wear a tie clip or a tie pin. It's better than flipping your tie over your shoulder. You could also try keeping your jacket buttoned with your tie in place when you sit. Or you could fold a napkin into your collar.

HATS

I normally don't wear hats—are there any occasions when I should wear one?

Hats, once ubiquitous, are no longer demanded at any social situation, and so differ from most other articles of men's clothing.

Today, a man wears a hat only for style, warmth or protection from the elements.

There are so many hats. Are their any classic hat styles?

Yes, there are innumerable varieties of hats. The United States, Britain and Italy are the hat-making centers of the world today, but hats these countries produce differ only slightly. Despite the many hats out there, they fortunately fall into a few classic species:

•**Fedora:** "The most classic shape in headwear history," states the catalogue of J.J. Hat Center, Inc., one of New York's oldest hat shops. The fedora appeared in the 1880s and quickly increased in popularity, especially in the United States. A fedora is, in fact, a term describing any felt hat with a *snapbrim* (a brim that is flipped downward in front). Fedoras come in numerous styles, such as the Como, the Lido, and so forth, each named by manufacturers according to the dimensions of the crown and brim and other details. With their soft look, fedoras have always been meant only for informal occasions or for business, but never for very dressy occasions.

Most fedora felt is made from wild hare or rabbit fur; but there is also wool felt, which is considered inferior. "Wool felt doesn't look as fine, it's not as supple, it doesn't hold its shape as well," says Mark Baum, manager of Worth & Worth, another of New York's quality hat shops. Beaver fur, once a common felt, has dwindled in use.

Two aspects determine the formality of a fedora's appearance: the width of the *ribbon* (hatband) and the width of the brim. The general rule is that the wider the ribbon, the dressier the look, with ribbon-widths ranging from about 1/4 inch to 2 inches. A wide brim "tends to be a little more casual," says Mr. Baum. Brims can be as wide as 3 inches.

The height of the crown has no bearing on the dressiness of a hat, but the shape of the crown, or "style of block," does. There are many crown shapes, but the most popular are (in descending order of formality): the *straight center-crease* (a front-to-back indent, which characterizes the homburg hat); the *teardrop* (the three-indentions that characterize the fedora); the *telescope crown* (a crown that narrows slightly toward the top); and the *porkpie* (a round, low, flat crown, favored by old-time jazz musicians, and which is too casual for wearing with a suit).

•**Homburg:** Although the homburg is a felt hat, it is not a fedora because it is not a snapbrim. The brim is rigid and curled up along

the edges, creating a dressier appearance than the softer fedora. The crown of the homburg has a single straight-crease, rather than the teardrop shape most common to the fedora. The homburg, named after the German spa town, replaced the top hat for England's and America's politicians and bureaucrats in the 1930s. It no longer is commonly worn, although it remains among the dressiest of hats and its moderate shape remains a classic.

•**Straw Hats:** There are several different types of straw hats, all meant for summer use:

Straw Boater
This round, flat-topped straw hat was popular at the end of the 19th century and early in this century, although now they have

practically vanished. They were first worn by British sailors, the story goes, then were taken up by young men at Britain's public schools, who wore them with blazers and decorated them with ribbons bearing school colors. The hat's popularity spread to America. Soon, it became acceptable to wear one with business attire. The boater remained popular until World War II, after which it vanished from most men's heads. However, straw boaters are still sold and can occasionally be spotted at festive, sporty events out-of-doors.

Panama

The Panama is simply a straw hat with a crown, brim and, usually, a ribbon. Genuine Panama hats, despite their name, are made in Ecuador. And although they are called "straw" hats, they are

made of a type of palm that grows in Central and South America. All Panama hats are hand woven. "The finer the weave, the higher the quality," says Mr. Baum. The quality is discerned from the suppleness of the straw and the fineness of the weave; the finer woven hats are made from the thinner strands of palm. The edge of a well-made brim is woven; a brim on a lesser quality Panama is folded over and sewn down over itself.

Panama hats became popular in the 19th century in the United States and Europe. The hat instantly became fashionable after a newspaper photograph of President Teddy Roosevelt, witnessing construction of the Panama Canal in 1906 while wearing a Panama, was widely reproduced. Many other famous men have worn the Panama, including Orson Welles, Humphrey Bogart, Gary Cooper and Winston Churchill. Panamas often have black ribbons, said by London hatmakers Lock & Co. to date back to the mourning of the death of Queen Victoria. But Panamas also are made with ribbons of brown or other colors, or with no ribbon. Some Panamas are made with a ridge along the top from front to back, which allows them to be safely folded and then rolled, for convenience while travelling.

Montecristi

The Montecristi is a type of Panama, but of craftsmanship so exquisite it deserves special mention. All Montecristis are hand-made in the Ecuadorian village that gave them their name. Good Montecristis can cost as much as a good suit. They are distinguished by the very small, fine weave of the palm, and are extraordinarily supple, yet durable.

•**Cap:** A soft hat with a visor, the cap emerged in the late 19th century as a popular hat for Britain's working-class men. However, caps eventually became  popular with the upper classes for leisure wear. Caps are made in lightweight summer fabrics and heavy wools for winter. They can have either a short or a long visor.

•**Beret:** A soft, round cap with no visor, this hat is associated primarily with the French, but berets are also worn in other coun-tries, such as Spain. A beret is often perceived, when worn by a man, as lending the wearer European, Bohemian air.

•**Top Hat:** A silk or beaver hat with a tall, cylindrical shape and flat top. It first appeared in Florence in the mid-18th century, and spread throughout the Continent and then to England, where it became the standard hat among gentlemen. According to legend,  the first man to wear a top hat in London, one James Heatherington, caused a riot, in January 1797, and he was arrested for causing a breach of the peace. But top hats soon became acceptable for daywear and formalwear. Since World War II, top hats have almost vanished. Even at white-tie affairs, top hats are rare, and are carried, rather than worn.

•**Bowler:** According to Lock & Co., a bowler is a stiff felt hat with a dome-shaped crown traditionally hardened by shellac. The

London hatter states that hat styles were once named after the man who first ordered one. But, in the case of the bowler, it was a farmer, Sir William Coke, who in 1850 requested a helmet-like hat be designed to protect gameskeepers from tree branches and other outdoor hazards. The hatmakers were Thomas and William Bowler, and  their name replaced Coke as the hat's name after the hat style became popular. In the United States, the bowler became known as the *derby*.

I like the look of a hat, but I'm afraid it will attract attention at my office—what is a classic and discreet hat style?

Yes, you will be making a fashion statement by wearing a fedora or another substantial hat, because hats (apart from baseball caps, caps and cowboy hats) are so seldom worn. So be especially careful to choose the proper hat for the occasion (no baseball caps to the formal wedding). Rely on knowledgeable sales staff at your local haberdasher to help you find the right hat until you feel confident enough to select your own headwear. As for which hat is a good, subtle hat to begin with, Mr. Baum, of Worth & Worth, advises: "Men should start off with a cap, which is less obtrusive than a fedora. But once you start wearing a hat, insecurity about it disappears very quickly and it feels very natual to wear. You may take a ribbing at first, but most men like the look."

Is it true that some men haven't the "right" face for a hat?

Any man will gain a bit of style by donning a good hat. The trick is to choose a hat style that flatters your face and physique, and that goes well with the rest of your clothes. "Everyone can wear a hat," says Mr. Kos. "You have to get comfortable wearing it and you have to be confident. If you're not confident wearing a hat, you'll look like a fool."

Men with a short, slight build will look best wearing a hat with a narrow brim and a crown that isn't too high, say experts.

Large men should wear slightly wider brims and a crown high enough to balance their heft. For a man with a round face, a medium-width brim and full crown would be best. Long, narrow face? Wear a low crown and narrow brim. Men with a regular-shaped face should wear a hat with a medium crown and brim.

But hat afficianados also warn against slavishly following such advice: "Limits are important, but the most important thing is that the person buying the hat feels confident in the hat," says Aida O'Toole, president of J.J. Hat Center. "If you start to put on restrictions—'I have a thin face so I have to wear a small brim, and I have to wear a lower crown'—you may start to look at hats and then restrict yourself and not try on something different. So the key is to go to a place that you feel comfortable with, where you can play with the shape of the hat. You have to be comfortable in your hat or you will never wear it." (Better hat shops will alter the shape of the crown to your specifications.)

Note that, today, crown heights are relatively uniform and shorter than they used to be, according to Mr. Baum:

"One of the first things people say if they're first-time hat wearers is, 'the crown is so high,' even though it's not so high. They're just not used to seeing something perched on top of their head. And they'll say the brim looks too wide, too. It does take a little getting used to."

Is my hat supposed to be coordinated with the rest of my clothing? If so, how?

Coordinate your hat, both its color and style, with your over-coat. "When a man is trying a hat on, it is best that he wears the overcoat that he wants to wear the hat with," says Mr. Baum. For warm weather, coordinate your hat with a suit or sport jacket. Don't match your hat's color exactly to that of your coat, which will create an overly synchronized look. It's better to select a hat of a color that agrees with clothes of other shades, too. Try gray, the color of dressy hats, such as the homburg, and also among the most popular colors for hats; gray works well with black and navy-blue coats. Equally versatile colors are brown, olive, tan and taupe (a shade of gray-brown). Black is also popular, although with a black overcoat it can look somewhat forbidding.

Choose casual hats to wear with casual clothes, dressier hats to go with dressier clothes; in other words, don't put on a cap with a three-piece suit. Caps, once the headgear of blue-collar workers, today are commonly worn by men of all walks of life. It is often worn with a sport jacket, but you should still think twice about wearing a cap with your dressiest clothes. Instead, try a fedora or a homburg.

Mr. Kos recommends that a hat should be chosen, above all, for itself: "A hat is almost like a friend. People get very protective of their hat; it's different than other articles of clothing. For that reason, you shouldn't worry about the color; get the one you like. There's no reason you can't wear a brown hat with anything."

How should a hat fit?

A hat should fit snugly, not tightly or loosely. Ms. O'Toole recommends the "shake test"—place the hat on your head and shake your head briskly. If the hat shifts, it's too loose. A hat "should be comfortable from day one," says Ms. O'Toole. "You should take a hat back if you're unhappy with it, even four months later—a good company will replace it." Mr. Baum adds further advice: "It should be snug but not uncomfortable. You shouldn't be acutely aware of it on your head. I suggest, when in doubt, err on the large side, because if anything, hats tend to shrink."

You may ask a salesperson to determine your hat size with a tape measure, but Mr. Baum suggests it's best to simply try on a hat. If you can't find a perfect fit, consider that, today, according to Mr. Baum, hats are shaped on standard oval blocks; at one time, however, there was a regular oval, a long oval and a wide oval for each hat size, in order to closely fit the shape of different head sizes. But the hat industry, faced with dwindling demand for its product in recent decades, now uses only regular ovals. "It is bad for the customer who doesn't fit in that mold," says Mr. Baum. "You would notice the difference if you were a really long oval."

HATS
30-SECOND QUALITY TEST

•**Felt:** The felt shouldn't be blotchy; it should feel supple. It should hold its shape when you crease it by hand.
•**Sweatband:** The sweatband should be made of leather, not cloth, and be sewn in; the lining, usually made of satin, should be sewn in, not glued. The brand label should be evident in the hat.
•**Edge:** Some hats have a "welted" edge—an edge that is folded then sewn down—which gives a hat a heavier look, but a welted brim is neither better nor worse than non-welted brims.
•**Lining:** Caps should be lined, and the lining of winter caps should be quilted, to provide warmth.
•**Bill:** The bill on a peak cap can be snapped or sewn to the cap fabric but the bill should be made of plastic so it will keep its shape.

How is a hat properly handled and worn?

First, how to pick up your hat. Don't lift it by the crown. With one hand, take hold of the front of the brim; with your other hand, take hold of the back of the brim. Place the hat on your head. "It is the most natural thing in the world for a man to grab a hat by pinching the crown and squeezing the life out of it," says Marc Williamson, manager of J.J. Hat Center. "That's the quickest way to wear a hat out. Ideally, you want to handle it by the brim to preserve the hat the longest."

There is no single correct way to wear a hat. A hat is properly worn both horizontal or angled to one side or foreward or backward for a jauntier appearance. The brim can be snapped down or not. "Everybody develops their own style for that," says Mr. Baum.

How should I care for my hat?

Hang your hat on a hook or a peg. If you lay a fedora on a flat surface, make sure to snap up the brim, which will help to preserve the brim's shape; or, turn the hat upside-down and rest the hat on its crown, because some brims won't bear the crown's weight. "Eventually, the brim is going to be like a pancake," suggests Mr. Williamson. For long-term storage, you should keep your hat in a hat box.

Also, brush your hat. You can do it yourself or ask a salesperson at a hat shop to do it for you. Hat brushes are made of horsehair, and are available at good hat shops.

"Brush in a counterclockwise direction, because that's the way hats are finished," says Mr. Baum. "They do have a grain," he adds. If you wear the hat every day, brush it once every two weeks yourself, or once a month at a hat store.

Brush your hat if it's been in the rain; if it gets thoroughly drenched, hang it and let it dry at room temperature, advises Ms. O'Toole. Alternatively, you can shake off any excess water, snap up the brim, and rest the hat on its crown on a flat surface.

Some experts recommend that hats should be steamed and *blocked* (shaped) once or twice a year. "A hat has a memory," says Ms. O'Toole. Or, you can hold it over a tea kettle while you brush the felt in a counter-clockwise direction.

How long will a well-made hat last?
Ms. O'toole says that a good hat will last three to five "seasons" (for example, straw hats are worn in the summer). Top-of-the-line hats can last 15 years, she says.

Am I supposed to tip my hat to a woman?
There is only one old custom that remains important to follow: a man should remove his hat when indoors. A hat, like a coat, is outerwear, and for the same reason that you would take off your coat once inside, you should take off your hat.

FORMALWEAR

A good tuxedo, of a fine fabric and with elegant tailoring, will make any man feel like royalty.
—Marshal Dutko, president, Baldwin Formalwear

The simpler, the better.
—Alfred Arena, associate chairperson, Menswear Design Department, Fashion Institute of Technology

E ach time you enter a black-tie affair, you sense the tuxedo's rich history. Formalwear can make an event magical and can transport us back to an era of more gracious manners. A "black tie only" invitation tells you that the event is important and usually one of celebration. The host asks not only for your company, but also for your willingness to participate in a traditional, formal occasion. By attending in proper attire, you show the host and other guests that you respect tradition.

The modern tuxedo is said to have been named after Tuxedo Park, New York, where in the 1890s a wealthy American, Griswold Lorillard, wore a coat without tails to a formal party. The style, which followed one that had been recently worn in England, broke ranks with the eveningwear of that era. The tuxedo dropped jaws at the time, but it has proven to be among the most enduring styles of the Western world: today's formal attire still includes elements more than a century old: the tuxedo, the tailcoat, the waistcoat and white-on-black austerity are all hold-overs of the Victorian era.

Sartorial customs applying to formalwear are more stringently adhered to than those applied to businesswear and casualwear, to the point of rigidity; so even if you wear a tuxedo only once, make sure you wear it correctly. This chapter introduces these customs and suggests how you may tastefully express your individuality.

How do "white tie" and "black tie" attire differ?

Black-tie attire is a slightly less dressy version of the regal white-tie-and-tails. Both are intended for evening events (after 6:00 p.m.), but today this rule is often disregarded. The following describes the main characteristics of both ensembles:

White Tie and Tails: White tie and tails is reserved for the most formal of occasions (e.g., weddings, soirees with diplomats, debutante balls and cotillions). "White tie is the highest level of evening attire," says Marshal Dutko, president of New York's Baldwin Formalwear. It is distinguished from all other attire by the black wool tailcoat. The coat's tails descend to the back of the knee, and the front of the coat is cut high at the waist. The lapels are peaked. A *waistcoat* (vest) with a peaked lapel is standard, and is never longer than the front of the coat. The waistcoat is worn over a stiff-fronted, wing-collar shirt of white *pique* (cotton or silk fabric woven to impart ribbed or waffle textures). The shirt sleeves have "link" cuffs which, unlike French cuffs, don't fold back over themselves. The shirt front is fastened by mother-of-pearl studs and cuff links. The bow tie, like the shirt, is white pique. Trousers have two black stripes, usually of satin or *grosgrain* (tightly woven silk or rayon fabric), down the outside side seams. The top hat was once part of the white-tie-and-tails outfit but is rarely seen today, and is usually carried rather than worn. White gloves and scarf along with a black overcoat complete the ensemble.

Black Tie: The tuxedo coat has no tails and echoes the relaxed lines of a smoking jacket, from which it allegedly derived. A proper tuxedo coat (also called a dinner jacket) is not vented because vents are a casual detail which would violate the formality of the tuxedo. It is made in three lapel styles, all with grosgrain or velvet *trimming* (the fabric used for detailing on eveningwear, usually on lapels, cummerbund and trousers). Most tuxedos are cut from black worsted wools, but some popular Italian tuxedos are made of silk and wool-silk blends.

The shirt traditionally has a wing collar, but a spread collar has long been acceptable. The shirt's front has eyelets for studs and French cuffs for cuff links. A single-breasted tuxedo is worn with a *cummerbund* (the wide, pleated, belt-like sash worn at the waist) or with a waistcoat (traditionally black), but never with both at the same time. A double-breasted tuxedo is worn without a cummerbund or waistcoat.

The bow tie is traditionally black, and made of the same satin or grosgrain fabric as the jacket lapels and cummerbund. Trousers are of the same fabric as the coat and have single black stripes of satin or grosgrain along the side seams and do not have cuffs, which would detract from the tuxedo's elegant simplicity.

How do "black tie" and "black tie optional" affairs differ?

If an event is designated "black tie," the most appropriate attire is a tuxedo, or your version of it. For an affair designated "black tie optional," it is never innappropriate to wear a tuxedo. If you are absolutely certain that most guests (and your companion) will be wearing relatively relaxed dress, you may opt for a conservatively cut suit in black, navy blue or dark gray. Wear it with a dark bow tie or four-in-hand and well-polished black oxfords.

Remember that being over-dressed is always preferable to being under-dressed.

What are the classic tuxedo styles?

The style of the coat lapel distinguishes one tuxedo from another (while a tailcoat has a peaked lapel). Tuxedos are also divided into those that are single-breasted and double-breasted.

Keep in mind that single-breasted tuxedos are customarily worn unbuttoned when standing; double-breasted tuxedos are, however, kept buttoned.

• **Shawl:** The shawl lapel has a rounded edge, and was allegedly the style of the original tuxedo coat, which was simply a formalized smoking jacket. With its soft, debonair lines, the shawl lapel is a classic on both single- and double-breasted coats. Jerry Haber, a salesman at J. Press, describes the shawl lapel as "timeless," but notes that the peaked lapel is "extremely popular and distinguished." The notched lapel is generally more popular on the East Coast, and "goes in and out of style, but is by no means improper," says Mr. Haber.

• **Peaked:** The peaked lapel of a tuxedo is essentially the same as the peaked lapel on a tailcoat or a suit, and its striking angles add flair. It may be preferred by those who favor the look of a double-breasted suit.

• **Notched:** The notched-lapel tuxedo is, in essence, a formalized single-breasted suit coat. It is considered bad form in some circles, because it is perceived as less formal and therefore less traditional, than coats with shawl or peaked lapels. Nevertheless, the notched lapel, despite its more recent vintage, has earned its place among the classics of men's formalwear. Most men appreciate its versatility. "The notched lapel gives men the most flexibility—it can be worn to business black-tie events as easily as to the opera," says Doug Rau, a salesperson at New York's A.T. Harris Formalwear Ltd.

I want the classic black-tie wardrobe. But I also want to add a bit of embellishment. How can I do so tastefully?

The classic black-tie ensemble may differ slightly from place to place, but whether it's worn in Los Angeles or in Natchez, Mississippi, the simple, elegant combination of black and white still predominates. Many men, however, say that an unadorned tuxedo is impersonal and uniform-like, and so choose to add a personal touch somewhere. Mr. Dutko, of Baldwin Formalwear, suggests that single-breasted tuxedos (either shawl or notched lapel styles) give men more room to personalize their ensemble, because they are worn with a cummerbund or vest.

It is perfectly acceptable to embellish your formal attire with imaginative colors, patterns and non-traditional fabrics, but experts recommend that flourishes be kept discreet. "I don't believe in introducing too much color with black tie," says custom suitmaker Jon Green. "It's the simplicity of the contrasts of black and white that makes it so impressive." Mr. Kalenderian, of Barneys, agrees: "Loud is not the answer; subtle is better," he says.

The black-tie ensemble has undergone much experimentation since at least the 1950s, when new colors, patterns and silk fabrications were introduced. It seems that each decade offers its own experimental and whimsical reincarnation of traditional tuxedos, usually with the aim of making them more casual. The most recent look has been wearing a black T-shirt or white band-collar fastened with a stud, with a peaked or shawl lapel coat. Once unthinkable, this approach has proven to have some staying power, especially on the West Coast. Some purists find the look grotesque; others think it handsome and balanced. One would be ill-advised, however, to mimic the attention-grabbing antics of Hollywood stars who are spotted at black-tie affairs in sneakers and baseball caps. This is alien to the spirit of formal dress.

The following describes the classic elements of the traditional black-tie wardrobe, then suggests how they can be tastefully modified to reflect your own style.

•**Coat:** The traditional tuxedo coats are those described above: shawl, peaked or notched lapel. These are single- or double-breasted and generally black. The double-breasted coat is just as acceptable as the single-breasted. Remember that a double-breasted coat is not worn with a cummerbund or waistcoat. One way to add a bit of panache is by foregoing black and selecting a tuxedo of midnight-blue, which has been around since the Duke of Windsor introduced it about 60 years ago. Midnight-blue tuxedos don't reflect artificial light as much black tuxedos do and therefore have, in fact, a deeper-hued appearance. A more daring alternative is to wear a dinner jacket with a pattern, such as a foulard or a paisley. But again, keep it simple. "Black tie really implies a black or midnight-blue tuxedo. With silvers, greens, yellows, you're beyond a tasteful level," advises Mr. Dutko. More daring still is to substitute a smoking jacket for the tuxedo coat. Do this only if you are supremely confident in your choice and how it will go over at a given function. It is safest to select a low-key smoking jacket—one of a solid color or with a subtle pattern. A classic summer tuxedo coat is a light-weight, ivory-colored, shawl lapel, worn with black or midnight-blue trousers.

•**Trousers:** Trousers are always black, with a single satin or grosgrain facing along the side seams. They are never cuffed.

•**Shirt:** The original shirt for black tie had a wing collar with a starched pique front. Later, a shirt with a less-formal spread collar and an unstarched, pleated front was introduced. Today, a shirt may have a plain front or pleated front. Spread collars are more appropriate with shawl lapels, because the soft lines of the jacket are complemented by the less sharply defined collar style. Wing collars combine well with peaked lapels because they echo the lapels' angularity. Shirts with quiet stripes, a simple check or a subtle window pane deliver some individuality.

Spread collar, plain-front   *Wing collar, plain-front*   *Wing collar, pleated front*

• **Shoes:** Formal shoes are traditionally black patent-leather opera pumps with a ribbed, matte-finished silk bow. Some men find these a bit dainty, and it is acceptable to wear alternatives, such as well-shined calfskin cap-toe oxfords, or black patent-leather or calfskin slip-ons. "I don't think pumps are that necessary, unless you're doing something ultra-formal," says Mr. Dutko. Avoid wing-tips, which imply business, or casual tassel or penny loafers.

• **Bow Tie:** Most men wear the black butterfly bow. But wearing a bow tie in a color other than black will not be frowned upon at many black-tie functions. If you venture beyond black, choose muted colors and patterns (e.g., maroon, navy, pin-dot or striped). Bow ties are generally of the same fabric as the lapels, such as satin or grosgrain, and are worn in front of the wing collar, which is said to have been designed to neatly prop up the tie. Note that the bat's wing and straight bow ties are just as acceptable as the butterfly for formalwear.

• **Hosiery:** The customary choice is black silk. They're still appropriate today, but finely woven black-wool socks are acceptable. A quiet pattern is not uncommon, but beware of venturing into colored socks, unless you want to make a bold statement. Whatever socks you wear shouldn't sag and bunch.

• **Waistcoat:** The formal waistcoat has a shawl lapel and three buttons, and is usually black. Waistcoats can be single- or double-breasted. To personalize your waistcoat, you might choose a muted check or paisley, for example. As with the cummerbund, avoid matching waistcoat to bow tie when you individualize it. Mr. Kalenderian suggests a waistcoat of a "beautifully woven fabric, such as silver-and-black" or micro-patterns in black and white. "Keep the pattern-scale small," he says.

•**Cummerbund:** The cummerbund conceals the trouser waistband—which is always unseen in formalwear—but cummerbunds are not meant to hold up your trousers. Suspenders are. The cummerbund, like the bow tie, is of the same satin or grosgrain as the coat lapels, and is worn only with single-breasted tuxedos. It is never worn with double-breasteds because it would be concealed. It also is never worn with a waistcoat. The cummerbund's folds are upturned—originally, it is said, to hold theater or opera tickets. The cummerbund is traditionally black, but you can personalize yours by wearing one of a different color or one that bears a subtle pattern. Choose a cummerbund that is of a different fabric or pattern than the bow tie; if they match, they will make your tuxedo look more like a costume or uniform and less like an expression of your personality.

•**Suspenders:** Suspenders are always worn with a tuxedo. They should be of white silk, and should button on, not clip on. You can individualize your suspenders by selecting those with a discreet pattern, such as pin dots.

•**Links and Studs:** Classic studs and cuff links are of gold or onyx, but studs and links offer a great way to personalize your tuxedo. Just make sure the studs and links are a set, or closely resemble each other. Jeweled links should be modest.

•**Pocket Handkerchief:** The classic pocket handkerchief is of white linen. But many men opt for some other style, such as a rich, dark, solid color, or an understated pattern, such as a dot or a houndstooth. A white silk handkerchief is also acceptable.

•**Overcoat:** The classic winter accompaniment to the tuxedo is a chesterfield overcoat with velvet collar, and a white silk scarf with tassels or fringes. Other dressy styles of dark coats will suffice. Raincoats are not considered appropriate formal outerwear.

•**Gloves:** Gloves should be gray, and of leather or suede.

•**Boutonniere:** A boutonniere is traditionally worn in the buttonhole of the left lapel. It should be a white gardenia or a red carnation, but few men wear them these days, says Mr. Dutko.

I'm getting married and am unsure which formal style to wear. What are some guidelines?

Customs clinging to formalwear for weddings remain strongly adhered to. The following (much of it offered by A.T. Harris Formalwear Ltd.) outlines some of these customs.

First, determine if your wedding will be formal or semi-formal, and if it will be held during the day or in the evening. Whether or not a wedding is considered formal depends on the bride's gown: if it has a train, the wedding is formal; anything else is semi-formal. A day wedding begins before 6:00 p.m. and requires the groom to wear a morning suit; an evening wedding starts after that time and requires the groom to wear a black-tie or white-tie ensemble.

The Stroller

•**Semi-Formal Day:** Wear a *stroller*, a dark-gray or black peaked-lapel coat, which is basically the day-time counterpart to the tuxedo. It is worn with a white shirt with turned-down collar; a gray or silver four-in-hand, a *Macclesfield* tie (wider than the four-in-hand and usually striped), or, rarely, a black or gray ascot. The vest commonly is gray or tan, and trousers are dark gray with black stripes. Shoes typically are plain black oxfords.

The Cutaway

• **Formal Day:** The main difference between semi-formal and formal day wedding attire is the style of coat. For formal weddings, wear a dark-gray or black tailcoat (also known as a morning coat) called the *cutaway*, which looks similar to the 19th century frock coat and is considered the day-time counterpart to the evening tailcoat worn with white-tie. The cutaway is worn with a wing collar; ascot tie (with pin); a tan or gray vest; and trousers of dark gray with black stripes. Shoes typically are plain black oxfords.

• **Semi-Formal Evening:** Any black-tie ensemble described earlier in this chapter is acceptable.

• **Formal Evening:** Wear the white-tie-and-tails described earlier in this chapter.

Should I buy or rent a tuxedo?

It depends on how often you attend black-tie affairs. If you wear a tuxedo at least three times a year, it may make economic sense to buy one—and perhaps two. "Renting a tuxedo is costly and it's much more sensible to have something at your fingertips," says Mr. Kalenderian. "Also, tuxedos, unlike suits and other articles in your wardrobe, don't need to be replaced to stay in fashion, so it is actually a long-term investment." If you can afford two, experts recommend owning one made of light-weight material for warm weather (perhaps a jacket of an ivory color) and one of a heavier weight for winter. If you own one tuxedo, it is best that it is of lighter weight fabric, which will suffice for all seasons.

Contrary to conventional wisdom, tuxedos don't have to

cost more than a suit, but a reputable rental store will charge you a significant amount for one night's use, and that doesn't come with a guarantee that you'll look elegant. Jason Phillips, a designer with New Republic, in New York, believes that a young man should own a tuxedo. "If you're twenty-six, spend all the money you can on a classic, black-and-white ensemble," he says. "When you have a beautiful tuxedo, you've got more room to be different. But looking different with a cheap, ill-fitting tuxedo doesn't cut it. Try to get a plain black topcoat, preferably of cashmere, and a scarf. Then, when you can afford it, start collecting more accessories, like a vest, a second shirt, and better cuff links and perhaps a stud set," Mr. Phillips says.

If you seldom attend black-tie affairs, then renting is probably the sensible path to take. Rented tuxedos often fit poorly, so find the best tuxedo rentals in town. Use your own cuff links and studs (or borrow a set), or personalize the tuxedo with your favorite pocket square.

I was once told never to remove my tuxedo coat. Is this advice correct?

Yes, you may take off your tuxedo coat—when you're ready to go to bed. Discarding your coat is a sure way to destroy the pomp of a formal occasion.

Salespeople

A good salesperson listens to his customer. And also has a knowledge of his merchandise.

—Paul Stuart

Men often base their dressing decisions on what they like to wear, not necessarily what looks best on them.

—Daniel Patrick Heaney, general manager, Sulka

When you purchase the classic clothes described in these pages, you will usually do so through a salesperson at a clothing store. Ideally, a salesperson will guide you to clothes that are elegant and well made. However, as noted in the preface, salespeople can be uninformative or overbearing, or both. The results can be costly mistakes. This chapter provides tips on how to know whether a salesperson is offering sound advice.

How can I tell if a salesperson is trustworthy?

"Good salespeople listen most of the time," says Mr. Heaney, of Sulka. "They should do a justifiable amount of talking with regard to specific answers to specific questions, but if they ramble on, that's not good; they're over-selling. A good salesperson is a good listener, who can determine the customer's wants and then guide them into that area."

So, in other words, you should do most of the talking. However, good salespeople may ask you questions, such as where you will wear the clothes, and so forth, to find the right clothes for you. Moreover, honest salespeople will tell you, without your even asking, if clothing is wrong for you.

"A good salesman will say in the fitting room 'this suit just doesn't fit you and you're not going to be happy with it after I've fixed it. Let's go try another one,'" says Mr. Pendleton, of Aquascutum. So, watch out for salespeople who insist that, with enough tailoring, the clothing will look fine. On the other hand, you should let a knowledgeable salesperson guide you. Like a good tailor, a good salesman can be enormously helpful; listen to his suggestions and gain from his experience.

MAKE SHOPPING A REGULAR THING

Learn how to shop. Too many wrong acquisitions are done from impulsive shopping. Ask around, find the most reputable shops in your area. Walk into the stores with confidence, don't be bashful, and don't let anyone push you into going into debt. Don't be embarrassed about your price range, and make that clear from the start. Know it's a learning process, and try to maximize what Mother Nature gave you. The major problems with most men's wardrobes is that men simply don't know how to shop. Be aware that most good salesmen start at the top of the price range and work down. State your range right away. This saves everybody time. Some men think once they try the suit on, they're trapped into buying it. This is not at all the case. There's nothing wrong with trying something else on. Women do the opposite. They have no problem trying on everything. One of the biggest errors is not shopping regularly. Some men go to a trunk show and buy twelve suits, then won't shop for years. Shop regularly, and take advantage of legitimate sales, like on Labor Day, or at the end of seasons.

—*Luciano Franzoni, designer and men's fashion analyst*

How can I tell whether a salesperson is knowledgeable?

One way you can immediately tell whether a salesperson is knowledgeable about his merchandise is if he selects a jacket in your size without needing to ask you what it is, according to Mr. Pendleton: "The first coat he puts on you should fit you, whether it's a suit coat or an overcoat," he says. Don't be impressed by a haughty demeanor or a confidently expressed opinion. Try asking a few questions about clothing to which you know the answers, and consider what the salesperson has to say. And of course, observe whether the salesperson is dressed in a style similar to yours. If he dresses in a much more subdued or louder style, he may not be the best guide for you.

A salesman convinced me to buy a costlier suit than I had originally intended to buy. Was I taken in?

Not necessarily. While of course some salespeople will try to sell you a more expensive item simply for a larger commission, a good salesperson will also seek to sell you a better item because it is a higher quality garment. "A good salesman trades down," says Mr. Pendleton, because a customer will probably think the first item he tries on is good enough and will pass on the second, more expensive one. "You can always trade a customer down, not up. A good salesman will show the better item first."

Furthermore, a good salesperson often will seek to help you buy additional items of clothing to go with the one you bought—such as trousers to go with a sport jacket—not to make the sale but to be of assistance. "A good salesman will try to make a multiple sale," says Mr. Pendleton. "The salesman will walk you to the furnishings department to help you pick the shirts and ties to go with a suit—and that costs him money because he could have been selling a $1,000 suit while he's picking out a $75 tie for you."

Sometimes I'm given very little help by salespeople. What can I do to ensure attentive service?

Start by dressing well when you shop. Salespeople will be more inclined to spend time with you if they believe you're there to buy something rather than to just lounge around. Second, if you are with your wife or girlfriend, assert yourself quickly, so that the salesperson speaks to you, rather than to her. Women often do make men's clothing decisions, and salespeople know this.

Custom suitmaker Jon Green offers additional advice: "Go to one or two stores and get the same salesperson in each store over and over—they will become your advocate. They will take back things that are not right, and they will call you with special things that you might want to know about."

DRESSING WITH STYLE

The individual creates style; the industry creates fashion.
—George G. Graham, owner, George Graham Galleries

A well-dressed person's clothes look a little unplanned.
— Jay Kos, owner, Jay Kos Haberdashery

Dressing with style is not as simple as strolling into the priciest shops and buying the finest classic clothes—style can't be bought, only garments can. Nor is dressing with style as simple as rigidly following sartorial "rules"—such as maintaining a 1/2-inch of shirt-cuff extending beyond the jacket sleeve, or matching belt to shoes. There are no "rules" that guarantee the attainment of true style, as there are rules for motorists or for stockbrokers. Indeed, the so-called rules, and even classic styles, change over time: since the Victorian era, men's clothing has veered toward simplicity in tailoring and somber colors, but in earlier ages (and in the 1960s) men wore complicated, gaudy, peacock-like clothing. Some classics, as we've noted earlier, were born dramatically: the dinner jacket was a revolution; and the first man to wear a top hat caused a riot in London. Other styles gradually gained broad acceptance: the cap was worn by laborers before the upper classes began wearing them for sport; the modern suit, the uniform of the business world, was only after the passage of years considered sufficiently dressy for a businessman.

Moreover, the "rules" are inconsistent—for example, while simplicity is the hallmark of formality, the additions of cuffs and pleats are considered dressy flourishes to a man's trousers.

Therefore, because rules and styles change, and are not always consistent, it's useful to understand the underlying aesthetic principles of dressing well, which will provide you with a reliable basis for making an independent judgement on what is stylish, and what is not, in the face of changing fashions. Broadly speaking, as we discuss below, dressing with style is knowing how to put together clothes that harmonize not only with each other, but also with your circumstances and with your personality.

No book, however, can provide a complete education about how to dress with style, any more than a book can teach one how to ride a bicycle. Building a wardrobe and creating an individual style must be done by experimentation. Go into clothing stores often. Go to the very best; compare their merchandise with those in discount shops. Touch. Look. Ask questions. Observe well-dressed people and, equally important, badly dressed people.

The Building Blocks of Style

Are there broad guidelines for combining my clothes?

Yes, there are. Most broadly, what you seek to achieve is visual harmony from head to toe—and beyond. Your clothing also should agree with your surroundings and with your personality. A three-piece, navy, pinstriped banker's suit may be a miracle of tailoring but it may not be right for you or appropriate for your job.

To achieve that harmony, at least four aspects of your clothing require artful manipulation: *color, pattern, texture* and *line*. This means knowing when, for all four, it is best for clothing to *match* (that is, to share the identical shade of a color, for example); when it is best for clothing to *coordinate* (that is, to resemble but not perfectly match); and when it is best for clothing to *contrast* (or work in opposite directions, such as black and white; heavy and lightweight fabrics). For instance, you would match the color of your belt to that of your shoes, but you would coordinate the colors of your pocket handkerchief to those of your tie. And you would coordinate the weight and texture of your trousers' fabric to those of your sport jacket, but not match them. You also want the dressiness or casualness of your clothing to agree.

•**Colors:** If you want to create subtle color combinations, then you would *complement* one color with another—you might pair a navy-blue blazer with a powder-blue tie. Both are blue, but of different hues. If the navy blazer and tie matched one another exactly, it would create a dull appearance; complementing, or *echoing*, colors avoids this.

Colors can also contrast, which means that they differ significantly, such as a gold tie worn with that navy blazer. Contrasting colors are noticed from two blocks away, a mile down the beach. Two or three contrasting colors bring out the brilliance of each, and form an ensemble that is bold but doesn't overwhelm.

When combining contrasting colors, choose one as the *leading* (predominant) color, then select supporting, or accent, colors. It's best to choose no more than two supporting colors. A suit, for example, is always the leading color, and the supporting colors are the shirt and tie. In casual wear, the leading color can be the sport jacket; or if no jacket is worn, then the shirt; the supporting color can be the trousers and accessories, such as the belt, shoes or a vest. Formalwear is pure contrasting color, with black the leading color, and white the supporting color.

•**Patterns:** To successfully combine patterns, the most important point to keep in mind is that they should never squabble amongst each other. You can wear not only two, but even three patterns together, such as a tie, shirt and jacket with different patterns. The key to combining patterns harmoniously is that they should be different types (such as a pinstripe suit and a foulard tie) or, if the same type, then of different sizes (such as a bengal-stripe shirt and a pinstriped jacket; or a tattersall-check shirt and a window pane-check sport jacket). However, once you start mixing more than two patterns, combining them successfully becomes difficult.

Finally, the colors of the different patterns needn't match but should complement one another by picking up some shade of at least one color in each other. A navy-and-red striped tie might pick up the burgundy in the stripes of a shirt. And, of course, the colors of the different patterns may contrast with each other.

•**Texture:** As for the texture of clothing, you should complement weights. If you wear a cotton summer suit, for example, you would complement it with a tie of similarly lightweight fabric, say of cotton or of linen. The reason is that weight is seasonal, and it's senseless to combine summer- and winter-weight clothes.

Further, the *finish* of clothes (the degree of the roughness or smoothness of their surface texture) should also agree. The finish determines the dressiness of an outfit, and it sends conflicting messages to wear, say, a dressy, hard-finished suit and a casual, roughly-woven oxford shirt. But you can also contrast textures, which, as with colors, draws attention to each of them. If you wore a cashmere sweater under a leather jacket you would be emphasizing the former's softness and the latter's toughness. But remember that different textures communicate different things. Tweeds bespeak life in the country, for example, so you would think twice about contrasting that texture with a Sea Island cotton dress shirt, which suggests city business.

•**Line:** Finally, the lines of your clothing should also gracefully combine. Lines can be highly fitted, or they can be *soft* (loose). Dressier clothing is often, but not always, more fitted than looser clothing. You can successfully contrast lines by wearing, for example, a tan, merino-wool turtleneck, pleated flannel trousers and an uncontructed sport jacket. Here, the form-fitting turtleneck contrasts with the jacket's soft lines and the full drape of the trousers. Contrasting lines can work powerfully in small ways, too: the pocket square or handkerchief, for example, is a way of adding line to an otherwise flat chest area; a thrusting Windsor knot adds a depth of line at the neck; a bow tie's horizontal plane also alters the quality of line; a thick, woven leather belt creates a different line quality than a thin, cordovan belt.

Are there any tricks to simplify all this when I put together my clothes each morning?

Combining clothes becomes much simpler when they are put together in their order of importance.

Start by selecting the clothing that will be the foundation for the rest of your outfit, and combine everything to those clothes. If you wear suits or sport jackets, then they are the first items to choose. The colors, patterns, texture and lines of your suit or jacket will be the basis for those of your other clothing, such as your tie and shirt. After you've chosen your shoes, choose your socks and belt. Pick out a pocket handkerchief and suspenders after you've settled on your tie.

If you're unsure about how to combine color, pattern and other elements, then build your wardrobe with standard, solid colors, such as navy blue and gray, or subtle patterns such as pin-stripes or bird's-eye. A man who isn't confident about his choice of clothing, says Mr. Arena of the Fashion Institute of Technology, "is better off not experimenting too much with color and pattern, and staying with solid colors."

SOME SPECIFICS ON STYLE

How can I choose the right shirt to wear with my suit or sport jacket?

A general rule of thumb: your shirt's color should be lighter than that of your jacket or your suit. A shirt that's darker creates an unconventional look. If your shirt has a pattern, make sure it gets along well those of your tie and jacket, following the guidelines above. A blue or white shirt will go well with most suits and ties. But try a shirt that has a subtle pastel shade, such as the faintest hint of blue or pink, which can serve as a good background for the rest of your clothes.

What should my tie agree with?

Your tie should primarily coordinate with your jacket, but not strictly match. "If you're wearing a blue suit and it has the finest stripe of burgundy, [your tie] might pick up on that stripe," says Paul Stuart. Or, contrast colors: wear a red tie with a navy suit.

Your tie should also go well with your shirt. Generally, keep your tie darker than your shirt. Also, keep the textures of your fabrics in agreement. Don't wear a fine cotton shirt with a nubby wool tie. Note that you should coordinate suspenders and pocket squares with your tie, not the reverse.

FINDING THAT GOLDEN MEAN

There is a dressing-down in corporate America today. In simpler times, the suit was the acceptable uniform in most business and social situations, but often this is no longer the case. Many executives are totally bewildered when casual attire is stressed for a meeting or social event. On the other hand, in sportswear there is a departure from the jeans and T-shirt look. It appears that people today are looking for the "golden mean," or a look that is somewhere in the middle—relaxed, yet to some degree representing their corporate persona. So, where corporate America is dressing down, casual America is dressing up. People are looking for wardrobes that serve double duty and are more versatile. The recent success of the shirt jacket is great example; it is rapidly taking taking the place of the more traditional tailored sport coat and, in many situations, the suit. However, by using better wool fabrics and incorportaing more tailored details, this more casual approach allows the wearer to achieve the desired casual or relaxed look while expressing his appreciation for style and quality.

—*Charles McGlothlin, general manager and buyer, Facconable*

Help me combine my shoes and socks with my suit.

Start by matching your shoes, which are far more visible than your socks, with your suit. Your shoes should, as a general rule, be of a similar color to that of your trousers. So, for example, you'd wear black shoes with a blue or gray suit; brown shoes with a tan or brown suit. However, well-dressed men often wear shoes of contrasting colors with their suits, such as brown shoes with blue or gray suits. And of course, the formality of the shoe style should agree with the dressiness of your outfit. So you may not want to choose elegant cap-toe oxfords to wear with rumpled khakis.

Note that dressy loafers, such as those with tassels, are commonly worn with suits, but loafers were originally a casual shoe, and don't always agree with all suits, especially very dressy ones. Also, they may appear a bit dainty with full-cut suits.

Your socks should be similar in color to your shoes, to be safe. But they can also be coordinated with your trousers. So, for example, you might wear black shoes with a gray suit and charcoal gray socks rather than black socks. Any patterns on your socks should be connected by color with your tie, pocket handkerchief or suit colors, in order to accent your entire outfit.

If a man's wardrobe should change with the seasons, how does one go about making adjustments?

There's no need to undertake drastic wardrobe changes, but it is customary to adjust the colors of your clothes to the seasons. When it comes to fabric weights, you certainly should not wear heavy wools or suedes in summer, or linen or fine poplin suits in winter, as common sense will tell you. In spring and summer, you might brighten your colors to agree with the brighter colors of the season. Your business suits and jackets may shift from navy and charcoal grays to lighter blues and grays. In the fall, your colors may be more reminiscent of autumnal country colors, such as rust and gold. Wear medium-weight wool jackets and suits.

How do I dress casually—yet tastefully—at the office?

Unfortunately, there are few, if any, clear-cut guidelines for casual office attire, because no two offices are identical. However, there

---

DRESSING DOWN WITH STYLE

WAR, HOLLYWOOD & AMERICAN SPORTSWEAR: A BRIEF HISTORY

Sportswear as a category is definitely growing in this country. But it has a long history. After World War II, soldiers came home and moved to the suburbs and discovered a more casual environment than what they were accustomed to in the cities. They could wear shorts, blue jeans and sports shirts, and they liked it. At the same time, Hollywood was having a great influence on the popular styles of sportswear. The cowboy movies, from John Wayne to Robert Redford, did a lot to make the rugged American look more acceptable, hence the overwhelming popularity of denim. The Hollywood of the 1940s—[with stars] like Jack Benny and Bob Hope, who are three certainties: your clothes should be clean and pressed; you should dress roughly in the same style that your superiors dress, though probably not much better; and it's preferable to be overdressed than underdressed.

The general principles that apply to dressy attire also apply to corporate-casual attire: harmonize color, texture, pattern and line. And of course, your overall appearance should harmonize with the atmosphere of your office, and your place in it.

Achieving this harmony can be difficult, because combining business clothes with casual clothes is a sartorial feat: it forcibly marries dressy attire with casuals. A bit of advice: avoid extremes. Jarlath Mellet, of Brooks Brothers suggests for example, a cashmere sport coat, merino-wool polo shirt and lightweight flannel trousers as a solid casual outfit for the office.

Suits: Dress down your suits by wearing them with sweaters or polo shirts rather than dress shirts. Only suits with soft silhouettes can make this adaptation well, because their more tailored-looking counterparts simply cannot shed that dressier look that comes with padded-shoulders, peaked lapels, darting, and so forth.

---

wore tailored sportswear—represented the golden era of casual dress. They showed how one could look relaxed but really sharp at the same time. One powerful example of how movies affect our outlook on what's right or wrong is when Clark Gable, in *It Happened One Night*, took off his shirt and exposed his bare chest. He had no undershirt! Immediately, undershirt sales plummeted. People thought, 'If he doesn't wear one, then why should I?' So, movie stars have a strong influence on how we dress. We look to them for signals.

These days, being well dressed in casualwear means looking comfortable. Jerry Seinfeld, I believe, is one of the best casual dressers in our popular culture. It's simply because he looks so comfortable in everything he wears. It fits well, and it suits his personality. You feel comfortable just watching him. That's the secret.

—Jack Herschlag, executive director,
National Association of Men's Sportswear Buyers

Pocket Handkerchiefs: If your office isn't especially casual, and requires a jacket, then perhaps a handkerchief—maybe casually tamped into the breast pocket, rather than folded—is a way to liven up your ensemble. However, handkerchiefs work best with a tie. If you go without a tie, you may choose not to wear a handkerchief.

Shoes: Shoes should be neither dressy, business-style brogues, nor sneakers, which are too casual for most offices. Go in the middle with a tassel loafer, for example, or with a buck oxford.

Shirts: Try shirts with more casual, countryish patterns, such as tattersall, and ties with a rougher weave. Or try a polo shirt, turtleneck or mock turtleneck.

Sport Jackets: Any of the classic Harris, Donegal or Shetland tweeds offer great flexibility for coordinating with casual clothing. Also acceptable are sport jackets of cashmere, camel hair and corduroy. And, of course, there's always the classic blue blazer.

What are the classic sweater styles? I'm looking for one that's versatile enough to wear at the office.

The most popular classic style is probably the the *V-Neck* (a pullover sweater with a V-shaped neckline), but it isn't the only style of knitwear you should have on your closet shelf. The *polo* sweater (a pull-over sweater, usually with a collar) with two or three buttons has been a classic for decades, and is especially elegant in merino or cashmere, and is highly versatile in neutral colors, such as dark gray or navy. Other standards include: the cable or ribbed

CASUAL FRIDAYS: YOU'RE AT WORK, NOT MOWING THE LAWN

Casual Friday has created monsters, and many companies are now suggesting guidelines, because the dress was over-the-top in its informality. Some men started a little too casual, wearing cut-off jeans, soiled pants—some went to the office as though they were about to do the lawn. I've had a lot of feedback from companies, who say that Casual Friday began as a debacle but that now employees are dressing up a little and striking a compromise, wearing elegant, informal attire. Acceptable solutions may be a black T-shirt or turtleneck with a blazer. In this way, you can strike a balance between looking elegant without appearing so stiff or ostentatious.

—*Luciano Franzoni,*
designer and men's fashion analyst

crewneck (a sweater with no collar and a high neckline); the *turtle-neck* (a pull-over sweater with a high, closed collar) made with either a *full-neck* collar (turned over) or a *mock* collar (a shorter collar that can't be turned over); and the *cardigan* (a button-down sweater with a shawl-like front). Keep in mind that turtlenecks and polo sweaters should be tucked in.

Just as important as a sweater's style is the type and quality of the sweater's material. *Cashmere* (hair of the Cashmere goat, originally from the Himalaya mountains) is one of the most expensive sweater materials, and its fine fibers create its famous, luxurious knitwear. *Merino* wool (the fine wool of the merino sheep, comparable to cashmere) is also in high-quality knitted fabrics. *Shetland* wool (a lightweight wool) and lambswool are fine for sweaters with ribbed or cabled weaves. Cotton is a perfect choice for summer knitwear.

Well-made, classic sweaters can be worn with or without a sport jacket, and can serve to both dress up and dress down an ensemble. And it might serve you well to wear thin 2-ply knits, which are comfortably worn under a sport jacket. As with other articles in your wardrobe, it is preferable to have a well-made classic item than several poorly made ones of trendy styles. Cheap sweaters age poorly: their colors can run or fade; they can lose their shape at the wrists and waist; and they can collect *pilling,* the fuzzy balls of loose fibers, more quickly than high-quality sweaters.

I've noticed that a "countrified" outfit is a popular look, but is it appropriate for the city?

The wardrobe—real or imagined—of the British country gentleman is the basis for a popular casual-yet-dressy look, which is acceptable in more and more offices. Many of the clothes are classics originally meant for outdoor sports, such as hunting, and often have sturdy fabrications, fastenings and many roomy pockets. Re-

---

TOWN & COUNTRY

Orvis, established in 1856, is one of the oldest makers of fishing tackle and sportswear in the United States. Its long list of customers include Dan Rather, George Bush and General Norman Schwarzkopf. Tom Lenz of Orvis explains why men turn to the country-gentleman look for weekends as well as during the week:

We carry lifestyle, or country, clothing, much of it intended for fishing, hunting and equestrian sports. It just so happens that many of these sports had British roots, so some of our sports clothing reflect British design and tradition. There's a practicality to wearing outdoors clothing. It's durable, protects against the elements, and allows for movement. It's good for those people who live in a fast pace but need to stay dry and warm. With the dress codes relaxing, we're seeing men go to the law office in more outdoorsy outerwear, like the Barbour coat. But then there's a limit one has to observe. Why would you need briar pants in New York City? I'm not sure how to answer, but men are doing that. But I think it stems from a desire to project a relaxed country confidence, even in the city. This look, for Orvis, anyway, could mean a Harris tweed, good corduroys, wool shirts with woven sportsman's motifs, plaids, and maybe a tie with a dry fly pattern. And men also want to be comfortable. Most men want to feel and look comfortable and rugged, even in an office building.

—*Tom Lenz, buyer, Orvis Ltd.*

cently, these outdoorsy items—the dominion of sportswear purveyors such as Orvis, Abercrombie & Fitch, L.L. Bean and the like—have become more acceptable for casual days at the office and for weekends, even in the city.

These classics include the pea coat and duffel coat, suede jackets, tweed and flannel sport coats as well as waxed-cotton coats and jackets popularized by Barbour. Also, wool and *Viyella* (a wool-and-cotton blend) shirts of plain colors and classic plaids are perennials. Shirt-jackets are being updated in more luxurious fabrics and sophisticated detailing. Trousers made of rugged fabrics, such as cavalry twill, moleskin, gray flannel and heavy cotton twill, serve a stylish, casual wardrobe superbly.

I supervise several people in my office. How should I dress in relation to them? And what should I wear on casual-dress days?

In most corporate and business climates, if you're the boss, it's important, even on casual days and at corporate outings, to dress like the boss. "Even if it's Casual Friday, I still want to see my

---

DON'T BE THE RENEGADE

Casual Friday can help in some environments, because some people work better in more comfortable clothes and show a more spirited morale. But the flip side is that other people work better in a more structured environment with a suit and tie. Things that are to be avoided on Casual Friday are sweatshirts, sneakers, shorts, tattered jeans and athletic T-shirts. Above all, don't follow the office renegade. This can be dangerous. Be safe. Often, people really don't know what kind of image they are projecting and how much risk is actually involved. Dress is very important in conveying sincerity and authority and gaining trust, so keep your eyes and ears open. There is always an unwritten code of dress everywhere and, as you rise in your profession, people will give you clues if you are making mistakes in your dress. Sometimes these are ever so slight and even disguised. Something said with a chuckle can be deadly serious.

—*Frederick Knapp, image consultant, Frederick Knapp Associates Inc.*

bank manager dressed better than the tellers," says Jason Phillips, of New Republic. Mr. Phillips offers some suggestions on how to dress casually, yet elegantly:

> Instead of a T-shirt, you can wear a French-cuff shirt or a fine sweater-vest. That hierarchy should still be recognized, even in casual dress situations; there still has to be some sense of authority. The answer is to have a sophisticated approach to sportswear. That can mean a linen pant with a polo shirt or turtleneck. The white, French-cuff shirt is the most versatile shirt you can wear—even with a $20 pair of chinos. The right pair of links can be the right touch to distinguish you from everyone else out there on casual days. And it doesn't necessarily look stuffy; it shows your sense of style. With menswear, there are so few choices, so it's so much more about the details.

Mr. Phillips adds that many men buy casualwear more discriminatingly as they get older:

> As most men get older, their eye matures, and they start gravitating to more classic, high-quality wardrobes. They're not involved with the same old dumb chino every morning. They might get the same chino design, but now it's wool gabardine, not cotton twill. If you're going to have one truly great piece of clothing, you might as well have the best. Instead of fifteen pairs of mediocre pants, get five great pairs. That hasn't always been the way the average American thinks. Wear less and better.

A FEW FINAL THOUGHTS ON STYLE

I've long thought that Cary Grant was among the most stylish of men. How can I look like him?

The answer is you can't. No matter how handsome or debonair you are, you are not a Hollywood film star from days of yore. The world is different now and so are men's clothes. But most important, you are unique, and while it is instructive to look at the attire of stylish men—such as Cary Grant (or, for that matter, Fred Astaire, Gary Cooper, the Duke of Windsor, other giants of 20th century style)—you should adopt what you admire about these men to fit your personality.

Mr. Kabbaz, a custom shirtmaker who made shirts for Cary Grant, explains further:

> You don't want to imitate a specific person on a consistent basis. You may admire how a few people look. But if you're going to copy, then analyze what it is about that person that you like. Is it Cary Grant? What you're really liking is the charisma, and there's no way it's going to happen. Cary Grant's style came from his ability to combine clothing to fit his personality. Style doesn't come from combining a wine-colored shirt with a navy tie and an appropriate blazer and trouser.

In other words, you can copy another man's clothes, but not his style. Each man must create his own signature style. "Style is knowing what you can wear, what you can pull off, what looks really good on you," says Karen Albano, a sales associate at Robert Talbott. "And adding your own twist to pull it all together."

Mr. Tucker, of Burberrys, agrees: "I can buy something and you can buy the same exact thing, and you will look different because it all comes down to style."

All right, I'm not Cary Grant. How can I find the best style for me?

Men who dress with a signature style usually know *who* they are and project a consistent image with their clothes. Mr. Kabbaz offers some advice:

> You don't necessarily want to be different; you want to be consistent. You can come up with five or six or seven different looks that look good on you. The question is: Who are you? Which look do you like the best? And once you figure that out, stick with it. People want to know who you are, and if one day you're wearing a double-breasted suit with a triple-starched, spread collar and a double Windsor knot and French cuffs, and the next day you come in wearing an unconstructed

Giorgio Armani jacket with baggy pants and loafers—then people don't know you, they know your clothes. People like comfort—the comfort of knowing that in the pecking order, you're *there* and they're *here*. If you can dress worse than them one day, better than them the next day, they're confused. They don't know who they're dealing with. I'm not saying you can't have more than one look or more than one life. For me the most important single thing is, once you settle on it, stick with it.

Also, don't wear so much finery that you become merely a mannequin for your clothing.

"Keep your dressing simple," says James Mullen, co-founder of London's Thomas Pink shirtmakers. "Your clothes should be a backdrop for you as a person."

Mr. Heaney, of Sulka, elaborates on this:

To achieve style, you have to take some elements of classic men's fashion and reinterpret them to fit your individual style—and you do that through how you put those items together. The key is to stay understated; less is more. Some people think that style is: 'this jacket gives me style because it was a $4000 cashmere jacket.' That may say that you spent a lot of money on that jacket but it's not going to give you style. Style is taking that jacket and then redefining it to fit who you are as an individual. But also saying to the world: 'I can take something this expensive, and make an understatement with it.'

It seems hard to create my own style with so many rules. Is there a rule for when I can break or bend these rules?

Yes, there is a rule for how and when to break or bend the rules: you may turn rules around if you understand the rules you're breaking, and if you're breaking them for a good reason. Indeed, the best dressers often say there are no rules.

Manipulating the rules is where an individual creates his signature style, because your clothes should be a reflection of you, not of broad rules.

Breaking the Rules

There's no accounting for taste. If you have taste and style, then you can apply any collar style to any cloth. There's no rule of thumb about that. For instance, Fred Astaire often wore a button-down collar oxford shirt with a button cuff with a double-breasted suit. A handful of men have that amount of style and confidence to carry that off. On most men it would look inappropriate, because it would look as though they didn't know what they were doing, as opposed to a guy like Fred Astaire, where everything was premeditated, and it all worked, for one reason or another. The guy had great style, had all his clothes custom-made—right to the length of his trousers, which were on the shorter side, to show sock color. What he did very successfully, in taking all these general rules and bending them, was emphasize an overall appearance and great style, for a slight, not very attractive guy, but a tremendously elegant guy. Whereas a guy like Cary Grant, who was disturbingly handsome and six-foot-one, used clothes as a backdrop to his good looks. He never wore things that drew attention to themselves, because you can imagine the combination of overt clothing with this good-looking guy—it wouldn't make sense. So, you have to find out who you are if you're really interested in clothes as an expression.

—Robert Gillotte, bespoke manager, Turnbull & Asser

If you think back about style, you think of those who personified style, such as Cary Grant, Humphrey Bogart, the Duke of Windsor, John Kennedy. They're the ones who helped create style. If they were to do something different, there was such respect for their style that the classic was adapted to it ... style adapts without destroying.

—Gregory deVaney, CEO, Turnbull & Asser

You can break the rule if you have a sense of your own style. And you have to have an assuredness of yourself to do that. And if you do, most of the time it is acceptable. Yes, there are all the rules—that you shouldn't wear brown shoes with a blue suit sort of thing—I think all those rules have been broken and rules should be broken, because men's fashion has come so far today from twenty or thirty years ago, when the rules were made and were pretty much stuck to. Look at IBM as an example, or a bank. When you walked into a bank, everyone wore a white shirt or a blue shirt. Today, that's not the case—in many cases it's unfortunate. But we are living in a different age today, things are changing and a new millenium is coming.

—J. Stanley Tucker, senior vice president, Burberrys

Selected Bibliography

The following books were useful in gaining an overview of the topics we cover in this book. We urge readers who are interested in learning more to consult these writings.

—J.K., C.S.

Boyer, Bruce, G. *Elegance, A Guide to Quality in Menswear*. New York: W.W. Norton & Co., 1985.

Buchet, Martine. *Panama, A Legendary Hat*. Paris: Editions Assouline, 1996.

Cassin-Scott, Jack. *Costume and Fashion 1760-1920*. New York: Macmillan Company, 1971.

Chaille, Francois, and Jean-Claude Colban. *The Book of Ties*. New York: Abbeville Press, 1994.

Fenton, Lois, with Edward Olcott. *Dress for Excellence*. New York: Macmillan, 1986.

Flusser, Alan. *Style and the Man: How and Where to Buy Fine Men's Clothing*. New York: HarperStyle, 1996.

Gale, Bill. *Esquire's Fashions for Today*. New York: Harper & Row, 1973.

Gross, K.J., and Jeff Stone. *Men's Wardrobe*. New York: Alfred A. Knopf, 1998.

Jackson, Carole. *Color for Men*. New York: Ballantine Books, 1984.

Keers, Paul. *A Gentleman's Wardrobe: Classic Clothes and Modern Man.* New York: Harmony Books, 1988.

Lurie, Alison. *The Language of Clothes.* New York: Random House, 1981.

McGill, Leonard. *Stylewise, A Man's Guide to Looking Good for Less.* New York: G.P. Putnam's Sons, 1983.

Molloy, John, T. *John T. Molloy's New Dress for Success.* New York: Warner Books, 1988.

Schoeffler, O.E., and William Gale. *Esquire's Encyclopedia of 20th Century Men's Fashions.* New York: McGraw-Hill, Inc., 1973.

The authors would like to recognize those who contributed their time, expertise and advice during the research for this book.

Alexander S. Kabbaz
903 Madison Avenue
New York, NY 10021

Aquascutum
100 Regent Street
London W1A 2AQ

(USA)
680 Fifth Avenue
New York, NY 10021

A.T. Harris Formalwear Ltd.
11 East 44th Street
New York, NY 10017

Baldwin Formalwear
52 West 56th Street
New York, NY 10019

Barneys New York
Madison Avenue and 61st Street
New York, NY 10021

Barrie Ltd.
268 York Street
New Haven, CT 06511

Beckenstein Men's Fabrics Inc.
121 Orchard Street
New York, NY 10002

Belgian Shoes
60 East 56th Street
New York, NY 10022

Bergdorf Goodman
754 Fifth Avenue
New York, NY 10019

Brioni Roma Style
610 Fifth Avenue
New York, NY 10020

Brooks Brothers
346 Madison Avenue
New York NY 10017

Burberrys
Chatham Place
29/53 Chatham Place
London E9 6LP

(USA)
9 East 57th Street
New York, NY 10022

Burlington Coat Factory
1830 Rt 130
Burlington, NJ 08016

Edward Green
12/13 Burlington Arcade
Piccadilly , London W1

Faconnable NY
689 Fifth Avenue
New York, NY 10022

Fashion Institute of Technology
Seventh Avenue at 27th Street
New York, NY 10018

Luciano Franzoni
P.O. Box 138298
Chicago, IL 60613

Frederick Knapp Associates Inc.
280 Madison Avenue
New York, NY 10016

Garrick Anderson Sartorial Ltd.
108-110 West 18th Street
New York, NY 10011

Gentle Custom Tailor
220 East 60th Street
New York, NY 10020

George Graham Galleries
101 West 55th Street
New York, NY 10019

Harrison James
5 West 54th Street
New York, NY 10019

Hickey-Freeman
1155 Clinton Avenue, North
Rochester, NY 14621

Holland & Holland
31-33 Bruton Street
London WIX 8JS

(USA)
50 East 57th Street
New York, NY 10022

J. Press Inc.
262 York Street
New Haven, CT 06511

J.J. Hat Center
310 Fifth Avenue
New York, NY 10001

J.M. Weston NY Inc.
812 Madison Avenue
New York, NY 10021

Jay Kos
988 Lexington Avenue
New York, NY 10021

John Lobb Ltd.
9 St. James's Street
London SW1 A1EF

Jon Green New York
903 Madison Avenue
New York, NY 10021

Metropolitan Museum of Art
The Costume Institute Library
1000 Fifth Avenue
New York, NY 10028

National Association of Mens
Sportswear Buyers
60 East 42nd Street
New York, NY 10165

Neckwear Association of America
151 Lexington Avenue
New York, NY 10016

New Republic
95 Spring Street
New York, NY 10012

Orvis Ltd.
Historic Route 7A
Manchester, VT 05254

Oxxford Clothes
1220 West Van Buren Street
Chicago, IL 60607

Paris Custom Shirt Makers Inc.
38 West 32nd Street, Ste. 603
New York, NY 10001

Paul Stuart
Madison Avenue at 45th Street
New York, NY 10017

Robert Talbott
680 Madison Avenue
New York, NY 10021

Sulka
430 Park Avenue
New York, NY 10022

Thomas Pink
1 Hazelock Terrace
London SW8 4AP

(USA)
520 Madison Avenue
New York, NY 10021

Tiecrafters
252 West 29th Street
New York, NY 10001

Trafalgar Ltd.
310 Wilson Avenue
Norwalk, CT 06854

Turnbull & Asser
71 & 72 Jermyn Street
London SW1Y-6PF

(USA)
42 East 57th Street
New York, NY 10022

Vincent & Edgar
972 Lexington Avenue
New York, NY 10021

Worth & Worth
331 Madison Avenue
New York, NY 10017

About the Authors:

Josh Karlen
Mr. Karlen, a lawyer, is a legal and financial journalist. He was a correspondent in the Baltics for United Press International, Radio Free Europe and many other news organizations. He lives in New York.

Christopher Sulavik
Mr. Sulavik has spent most of his career as a journalist, including four years with Reuter news agency. He has contributed articles to *Newsweek*, *The International Herald Tribune*, *The European* and *The Christian Science Monitor*. Most recently, he wrote *NYC For Free*. He owns Tatra Press and lives in New York.